"What do

Matthew eyed her warily. But, despite his guarded demeanor, there was a strange sort of softness in his eyes.

Was that hope hiding somewhere behind his protests?

She was spared the agony of mulling over those questions when Matthew gave a curt nod and extended his hand.

"Okay."

Penny hesitated for just a moment before slipping her hand into his. The sudden warmth that resulted took her by surprise, drawing her gaze to their intertwined hands.

Oh, no... Hold it together, girl!

If she didn't, she'd end up melting like an icicle during the spring thaw.

Drawing in a quick breath, Penny steeled herself as best she could. She would not let Matthew Banks distract her. No matter how attractive he happened to be. This was a business arrangement, nothing more.

Now if only she could convince her racing heart.

Isabella Bruno has been writing stories for as long as she can remember—and she still has the grammatically-challenged grade school manuscripts to prove it! In addition to word-wrangling, faith, family and food are her greatest passions. When she isn't getting lost in a fictional town, Isabella can be found volunteering at ministry events, crafting at her sewing machine, and shamelessly spoiling her niece and nephews. You can connect with Isabella on her website, isabellabrunowrites.com.

Books by Isabella Bruno

Love Inspired

Her Second Chance Christmas

Visit the Author Profile page at LoveInspired.com.

HER
SECOND CHANCE
CHRISTMAS

ISABELLA BRUNO

LOVE INSPIRED
INSPIRATIONAL ROMANCE

If you purchased this book without a cover you should be aware that this book is stolen property. It was reported as "unsold and destroyed" to the publisher, and neither the author nor the publisher has received any payment for this "stripped book."

LOVE INSPIRED®
INSPIRATIONAL ROMANCE

ISBN-13: 978-1-335-62118-4

Her Second Chance Christmas

Copyright © 2025 by Isabella Bruno

All rights reserved. No part of this book may be used or reproduced in any manner whatsoever without written permission.

Without limiting the author's and publisher's exclusive rights, any unauthorized use of this publication to train generative artificial intelligence (AI) technologies is expressly prohibited.

This is a work of fiction. Names, characters, places and incidents are either the product of the author's imagination or are used fictitiously. Any resemblance to actual persons, living or dead, businesses, companies, events or locales is entirely coincidental.

For questions and comments about the quality of this book, please contact us at CustomerService@Harlequin.com.

® is a trademark of Harlequin Enterprises ULC.

Love Inspired
22 Adelaide St. West, 41st Floor
Toronto, Ontario M5H 4E3, Canada
www.LoveInspired.com

Printed in Lithuania

Recycling programs for this product may not exist in your area.

MIX
Paper | Supporting responsible forestry
FSC® C021394

Trust in the Lord with all thine heart; and lean not unto thine own understanding. In all thy ways acknowledge him, and he shall direct thy paths.
—*Proverbs* 3:5-6

All glory, praise and gratitude first of all to the God who inspires every love story, both real and imagined. Special thanks also to my beautiful mother, who has been gleefully devouring my work ever since I was first bitten by the romance bug back in grade school.
Thank you for always being my biggest fan.
I love you more than these frail words can say.

Chapter One

It was like something out of a Christmas movie.

At least that's how Penelope Shay felt as she slowly drove through a stretch of festively lit homes leading into Cedar Ridge, Michigan's main strip. Between decorative wreaths hanging grandly on front doors, lit-up evergreens adorning lawns like gigantic ornaments, and more inflatable Santas than she could count, Penny didn't know where to look first. Even the weather was getting in on the act, raining down fat, fluffy snowflakes that lightly dusted the ground, lending an even more wonderful feel to the otherwise Christmas-happy town.

Penny released a poignant sigh, disappointed but not surprised when the emotion-laden release failed to alleviate the effects of her ongoing internal war. Hometown comfort and newfound grief continued to vie for supremacy within, and Penny was caught in the crossfire.

"So...?" Morgan Thompson's voice, sounding over the car's speakers, broke her out of her reverie. "Don't keep me in suspense. What's your big surprise?"

Penny reached for a knob on the dashboard to lower the volume in anticipation of her best friend's reaction.

"I accepted Andrew's offer."

"Are you serious?! You're moving back too?!"

"Driving down Main Street as we speak."

The delighted shriek that sounded on the other end of the

line burrowed deep into Penny's heart, tapping into a wellspring of mirth that erupted into boisterous laughter. After the week she'd just had, it was exactly what the doctor ordered.

Well, that and open-heart surgery. But that would have to wait for now.

"Penny!" Morgan squealed. "I can't believe this! What happened to change your mind?"

Penny sighed again, this one substantially wearier.

"Nick broke up with me."

And that was just the tip of the iceberg.

"What?" Morgan exclaimed. "I thought things were going well with you two! What happened?"

Hypertrophic cardiomyopathy, that's what.

Penny wasn't unfamiliar with the scientific term for thickened heart muscles, but this was the first time it had been applied to her. When the symptoms first began to manifest themselves, Penny waved them off, not wanting to even consider the possibility that she had inherited the same condition that took her mother's life eight years ago. For months, she explained away the unusual fatigue, dizzy spells, and lightheadedness as overexertion. But after nearly fainting on her morning commute two weeks ago, she knew she couldn't put off seeing a doctor any longer.

Arriving at her boyfriend's apartment in tears following the diagnosis hadn't made things any better. Far from the sympathy and compassion she had expected, Penny had been met instead with withdrawal and rejection.

I'm sorry, Penny, but that's just not a risk I'm willing to take.

"Did he at least tell you why?" Morgan asked, eager for details.

"He said he couldn't see a future with me in it," Penny replied, her voice a dull monotone.

Talk about heartless! Her hands tightly gripped the wheel

at the memory. A heartless response to a heart condition. How was that for ironic?

"I'm sorry, Penny," Morgan said, her voice sympathetic and soft. "You deserve so much better than that."

"Thanks," Penny said quietly, pausing for a moment.

"Have you seen your brother yet?" Morgan asked.

"I just arrived, so not yet," Penny replied truthfully, opting to heed her friend's request. "But I'm hopeful that the Returning Residents program will be the fresh start we both need."

The program in question was an ambitious revitalization project that had been set up in Cedar Ridge, Michigan. As a small farming community with only a few secondary businesses, the little town didn't have much to offer its high-school graduates. As a result, most tended to leave to pursue higher education and career opportunities in larger cities across the country. The elderly mayor Steven Bennett, disheartened by the town's shrinking population, now hoped to reverse that trend by offering grants to former Cedar Ridge residents willing to return to their hometown to start new businesses. Penny's younger brother, Andrew, had taken advantage of the opportunity to open a bakery, a dream that both siblings had once shared with their mother.

To say that the two had handled her death differently would be a severe understatement. While Andrew had found comfort in the memories that lingered in their hometown, Penny felt as though she was being smothered. At any moment, remembrances could reappear, interrupting an otherwise normal day and sending her down a spiral of overwhelming grief. At that time, Cedar Ridge had felt more suffocating than secure. So when her uncle suggested that the two of them might come live with him in upstate New York, Penny had jumped at the chance. But Andrew had other ideas.

Her thoughts stopped short as the steeple of St. Jude's Church came into view. When Penny had made the decision to come home, she had expected a confrontation with the memories of past Christmases, but seeing the white clapboard building that stood proudly at the center of town struck Penny with a force she hadn't been expecting.

This was the same church that Penny had attended with her family every Sunday for the better part of her twenty-five years. The same church where she'd had all her grade-school recitals. The same church that she envisioned anytime her thoughts strayed to the idea of marriage...

Marriage. Would she ever know the feeling of being loved, really and truly, for who she was?

Penny shook her head as if to clear it of such troublesome thoughts. There was no use dwelling on things she had no control over.

"But now that you're back," Morgan continued. "Can I ask you a favor?"

"Sure."

"Would you mind stopping by my shop to check on its progress? I haven't heard anything from the builder in weeks and I'm starting to worry."

"No problem," Penny agreed. "I'll go tomorrow."

"Thanks," Morgan said. "I really appreciate it."

Penny barely saw the scenery as her car continued its steady path toward home, so familiar were the roads. Soon enough, she was pulling into her grandmother's driveway and parking beside a large black pickup. She got out and retrieved her suitcase from the trunk, wincing as a sharp pain sliced through her chest. The heavy luggage dropped to the ground with an unceremonious thud as she pressed a shaky hand over her heart. Her lips twisted in a grimace spurred by equal parts pain and shame.

She was going to have to be a *lot* more careful from now on.

The reality of life with a heart condition was still something Penny was getting used to. After living independently in New York City for so long, she wasn't accustomed to asking anyone for help.

Not that she'd be able to do that here, either.

Nick's rejection had brought things into sharp focus. Prior to her diagnosis, he was the perfect boyfriend. But as soon as he heard the news, he'd changed. Like a light switch turning off, his interest—not to mention his compassion—suddenly ran dry.

That's not a risk I'm willing to take.

How would Penny's family and friends respond to her illness, especially considering what it had done to her mother? Would they avoid her out of fear? Would they pity her and handle her with kid gloves? Penny didn't know, but she wasn't interested in finding out.

Still, she thought, straightening as the last of the pain subsided, it would be nice to have someone to lean on for support. Or at the very least, to carry her luggage.

But Penny's heart condition made her a liability. A risk. No man wanted to marry a woman whose future wasn't guaranteed. She had learned that the hard way.

The truth was, Nick was right. Dating her was a recipe for heartbreak. It didn't make what he did any easier, but after losing her mother so suddenly, Penny could at the very least understand his motivation, even if she didn't like it.

Trudging through a fresh layer of snow, Penny dragged her hefty suitcase across the fieldstone walkway that led to the front door. Thankfully, there were no stairs leading to the entranceway of the stately Colonial house, just one small step up to a covered porch.

Once on the landing, Penny drew in a deep breath of crisp winter air, pausing to gaze up at the stars that dotted the darkened sky. She felt a bittersweet smile tugging at the corners of her lips. Stars always made her think of her mother. Elizabeth Shay could name every constellation known to man, and also a few of her own invention. Stargazing had been a favorite activity of theirs, right up until the moment when...

"Good night, Mrs. Nesbitt."

The words barely had time to register before the man who'd said them collided with Penny.

"Whoa, sorry!"

Penny stumbled as she tried not to fall over her luggage. Thankfully, two large hands reached out and pulled her close—very close.

Penny closed her eyes as she fell into her rescuer's arms, mortified at what was happening. With the only light coming from the small twin sconces that framed the front door, the winter evening would—hopefully—hide the blush she felt creeping up her cheeks.

"Are you all right?"

That low voice sounded *very* familiar.

The man stepped back just enough so that he could look at Penny, and her worst fears were confirmed. Matthew Banks—who was once the most eligible bachelor of Cedar Ridge, and the focus of her high-school daydreams—was looking down at her, a concerned expression softening his rugged features.

He was waiting for a response, but Penny didn't trust herself to speak while gazing up into those impossibly green eyes. She was far too busy trying to restrain a dreamy sigh from escaping her lips.

How was it possible that Matthew had become even *more* attractive since high school? He had always been boyishly handsome, with his sandy blond hair, emerald eyes, and easy smile, but now, sporting a shorter haircut and a day's worth of stubble, he looked as if he'd just stepped off a magazine cover.

"Penny?" Matthew's perfectly chiseled jaw went slack as he recognized her. "What are you doing here?"

Trying real hard not to swoon.

"Starting over," she answered, pushing the words through a suddenly parched throat.

Penny bit the inside of her lip to keep an amused smile from escaping as twin furrows appeared on Matthew's forehead. After the way she had taken off midway through her junior year without a second glance, she would likely be seeing this confused expression on more than a few faces around town.

"I…" Matthew seemed at a loss for words. Then he found his voice. "You're a returning resident?" Matthew asked finally.

A sharp stab of regret hit her hard, her rapidly beating heart reminding her of the real reason she'd come home.

"No, no," Penny hedged, ducking her head and taking advantage of the opportunity to put some space between her and Matthew. "My brother is opening a bakery. I'm just here to help him with the business side of things."

"Oh." Matthew shoved his hands into his pockets, still looking less than comfortable with her unexpected appearance. "You're good with that sort of stuff?"

"I was an executive marketing director back in New York." Penny pressed her lips together when she heard how snobbish that statement sounded. She hadn't meant to brag.

Matthew leaned back on his heels and let out a low whistle. "Wow. Impressive."

"Not really." Penny shrugged, darting her gaze down to the floor before forcing it back up again. She had worked hard over the years to overcome her painful shyness. She wouldn't let it overtake her now. "It's hardly rocket science."

"Might as well be to me," Matthew replied. "Websites, blog posts, hashtags…" A sly smile played at his lips as he leaned in conspiratorially. "I don't even have a social-media account."

Penny's jaw dropped. "You don't?"

Matthew chuckled, a deep sound that reverberated through

her like a subtle tremor before an earthquake. "I'm guessing that means you've never tried to look me up."

"I haven't kept in touch with anyone," she admitted. "Except Morgan."

A sympathetic sheen lent new depths to Matthew's captivating eyes. He knew full well that even if they hadn't been best friends since kindergarten, Morgan, who'd lost her own mother at an even younger age, would have been the best person to help Penny navigate life after loss.

"Best-friend privileges?"

Penny felt her lips quirk up into an almost-smile. "Something like that."

He nodded, holding her gaze for just a moment too long before turning to take his leave. "Well, I guess I'll see you around, then."

"Yeah." Penny released the word on a relieved breath. Hopefully, now, she could coax her heart rate back down to normal. "See you."

Catching sight of her big suitcase, Matthew stopped. "Do you want a hand with this?"

"No, thanks," Penny answered reflexively. "I'll manage."

Only when she heard the soft thud of his car door did Penny relax. She hadn't been back in town even thirty minutes, and already she had run into the one man who could jeopardize her newfound resolve to stay single. When making the snap decision to come home, Penny hadn't considered that her former crush might also be taking advantage of the Returning Residents program. To be honest, she hadn't considered much of anything. After her breakup with Nick, she just knew that she needed to run, and fast.

"I thought I heard voices out here!"

Penny's concerns quickly dissipated fast at the sound of her grandmother's cheerful voice.

"Nana!" Penny threw her arms around her grandmother's plump frame and held on tight. "I missed you!"

That was the truth. This homecoming was exactly what Penny needed.

If only it hadn't taken a life-threatening diagnosis to show her that.

"Let me take a closer look at you," Betty instructed as she pulled away. "Oh, sweetheart, you're even more beautiful than I remember!"

Penny beamed. What a typically Nana thing to say.

"I'm sure my handyman noticed, too." A mischievous twinkle brought her crystal-clear blue eyes to life as she gave her granddaughter a teasing nudge.

"Nana…" Penny groaned, feeling as though she'd been transported back to her teenage years. "You stop that right now."

"And if memory serves," Nana continued, completely ignoring Penny's request, "that's the same boy you were sweet on in high school, isn't it?"

Penny felt a familiar heat begin to rise on her cheeks. "Okay, that's enough," Penny announced. "Let's get inside."

With that, she grabbed her luggage and hauled it over the threshold. The action wasn't wise on her part, but she certainly couldn't ask Nana to help her. Not without alerting her to Penny's heart condition.

Nana's gleeful laugh followed Penny inside. It didn't surprise her one bit that her grandmother was excited by the prospect of a Christmas reunion. She adored soap operas, and was an eternal optimist, always hoping for a happy ending.

Releasing the suitcase, Penny paused to catch her breath. There was no way she was going to drag that monstrosity up the stairs, at least not tonight.

Turning around, Penny took in the familiar space, feeling the weight on her shoulders ease slightly. The floral wallpaper, the built-in bookcases boasting books of every size and shape, the impressive collection of family photos hanging proudly on the walls... Everything was exactly as Penny remembered, untouched by the hands of time.

This place was like a living time capsule, completely unchanged. And while the memories that filled these walls had initially driven her to leave, Penny was relieved to find that those same memories were now making her smile. There was a comfort in knowing that, no matter what Penny may have to face in the near future, home would always be here, waiting for her.

Time heals all hearts.

Penny's smile waned as she remembered one of her mother's steady refrains. Time hadn't healed her heart. But then, Mom hadn't been talking about physical healing, had she?

"I'm so glad we get to spend one last Christmas here together." Nana smiled, closing the door behind her.

Unease turned to dread as a cold shiver settled into her stomach, twisting it into an uncomfortable knot. There's no way Nana could know about her heart condition. But was she facing a health struggle of her own?

"What do you mean, 'one last Christmas'?" she asked, spinning to face her grandmother. Before Nana had the chance to respond, Penny caught sight of a real-estate brochure lying on the entrance table. "You're selling the house?!"

Penny's loud exclamation caused Betty to jump.

"Well, this big, old house is getting to be a bit too much for me to take care of," Nana offered, almost apologetically. "Andrew is staying in the apartment over his bakery, and I didn't know you were coming home, so..."

Penny closed her eyes and pinched the bridge of her nose. Neither had she.

"I found a smaller house closer to town," Nana continued.

"It's not far at all, and, of course, you're more than welcome to stay with me there."

But she knew it wouldn't be the same. This was where the memories of her mother still lived. If someone else bought it, things would change... And Penny wasn't ready for that just yet.

For what felt like the hundredth time since her diagnosis, Penny felt a strong urge to pray. But after years spent ignoring God, how did she know he even wanted to hear from her anymore?

"I mean, thank you for the offer," Penny said, switching gears, belatedly remembering her manners. "Does Andrew know about this?"

"Yes." Nana nodded. "And he thinks it's a good idea."

Penny's shoulders slumped. "Of course, he does."

"Oh, honey," her grandmother began, stepping forward to cup Penny's face with her hands. "I'm sorry this is so difficult for you. I didn't think it would be, given how you seemed to flourish in New York." She chuckled, trying to make light of the situation. "What would a brilliant business executive like you want with an old house like this, anyway?"

Her grandmother's voice, soft with empathy, shattered Penny's defenses and left her feeling like a child.

She didn't like it one bit.

Stepping away, she mentally scrambled for a solution. Yes, she may have wanted—even needed—something different years ago, but things had changed...drastically. Now, this home was exactly what she needed, and Penny wasn't going to let it go without a fight.

"How much do you want for it?"

Nana hesitated. When she named a figure, Penny's heart plummeted. She'd never manage to scrounge up enough money in time. Not with her upcoming surgery bill to be mindful of.

"I'm sorry, sweetheart," Nana said. "But try not to let it

ruin your Christmas. It's just a house, after all. We're together now, and that's what matters, right?"

Penny nodded, unconvinced. With nothing left to lose, she gave in and sent up a silent plea.

God, if You're out there, and if You still love me, I could really, really use Your help.

Matthew blew out a frustrated huff as the whirring lathe slowed to a stop. He had been turning a leg to replace the one that had rotted on his latest restoration project, but he'd botched it royally.

Again.

Sigh...

This was all Penny Shay's fault. Why did she have to waltz back into town and throw his world off its axis, anyway? It was hard enough keeping himself focused these days without the distracting memory of Penny playing on constant repeat.

Matthew ran a hand across his face and groaned. He couldn't very well fault her for returning home. She had just as much right as anybody to participate in Mayor Bennett's attempted town-revitalization project. But the shock of seeing her had shaken him badly. He never thought he would see her again, but now here she was, stirring up old feelings that he thought had disappeared a long time ago.

"Knock, knock."

Matthew turned to find his sister, Cassandra, standing in the doorway, holding two mugs of coffee.

"I don't remember you being an early bird," he joked, grateful for the distraction.

"Who can sleep with all this construction going on?" she teased right back.

"In my experience, when someone offers you a place to stay rent-free, you generally don't complain about their morning habits."

Cassandra released a quick laugh. "And have I mentioned how grateful I am to be living in your guesthouse?"

Matthew felt an odd pull in his chest at the word *your*, but he quickly shook it off. It had been almost a year since he'd inherited the land. He might as well get used to it.

Even though he'd spent nearly seven years working with Mac Conlin at Cedar Ridge Carpentry, the business he had started decades ago, Matthew had been totally surprised at the reading of Mac's will. His mentor left him everything, from his land to his home to his workshop and business. It was a gift he felt he didn't deserve. It was Matthew's fault Mac had died, after all, and he had spent the better part of last year trying to figure out how to make that right.

"Not since yesterday," he joked, mentally praising himself for sounding much more lighthearted than he felt.

His sister merely smiled as she handed him a steaming cup. But the glint that passed through her brown-eyed gaze told Matthew this visit was about much more than morning coffee.

"Well," she said, cradling her mug in both hands. "I just wanted to check in on you. I mean, now that Penelope Shay is back in town."

Ah, there it was.

"So?" he muttered, taking a sip from his mug to stop any more words from accidentally spilling out.

"Come on, Matt." Cassandra tilted her head, sending her long, dark ponytail swishing from side to side. "Are you really going to pretend that you don't care that she's back?"

Matthew shifted, setting the mug down as he surveyed his work, all the while avoiding eye contact with his meddlesome older sister. "Who's pretending?"

Cassandra didn't offer an immediate response, but Matthew knew better than to assume her silence was sympathetic.

She's just plotting her next move.

Even without her two best friends in tow—a group that Matthew had once affectionately dubbed the Little Miss Matchmakers—Cassandra was a force to be reckoned with. If he gave her an inch, she would take a mile. The best course of action was to just stand firm.

"Okay, okay," she finally conceded. "I get it."

Matthew clenched his jaw, lest irritation get the better of him. Dealing with Penny's sudden reappearance in Cedar Ridge was going to be hard enough. The absolute last thing he needed was his sister getting involved.

"Fine," she continued, turning to go. "I'll back off."

The *for now* was unspoken.

"What time did you want to head into town today?" she asked over her shoulder at the door.

"Might as well go now," he answered.

He sure wasn't getting anything accomplished in this frame of mind. It was time to switch gears.

"Okay," she replied. "I'll go grab my things."

Once Matthew was certain she was gone, he released a quick breath. First Penny, now Cassandra... What next?

Turning from the century-old wingback chair, Matthew walked over to a table situated in the corner of Mac's—er, *his*—workshop. Tiny shards of wood, stained in various natural hues, lay scattered around a large board, where Mac's last mosaic was still waiting for completion. Prior to meeting Mac, Matthew had never seen such a thing done before, but then, his mentor had been one-of-a-kind. Who else could use the scrap pieces of wood from his projects in such a remarkable way? Of course, Mac had never seen it that way. He'd always say he was just killing time.

If only you had gone instead of him...

Those accusations never seemed to quit. They hovered on the periphery of his mind, always waiting for an opportunity to taunt Matthew. But how could he have known the night Mac left to make a delivery would be his last?

If only he hadn't let the man go alone. If only he had been the one to make the hour-long drive northeast to Ann Arbor. If only Mac had seen that patch of black ice.

If only, if only, if only…

Matthew shook his head as if to dislodge the errant thoughts. Unfortunately for him, that never seemed to work. Sure, he could distract himself for a while—and he had been, running himself ragged keeping up with special projects on top of all the renovations for Mayor Bennett's new program. The mayor had hired Matthew to oversee the renovations of twelve storefronts on Main Street, along with the accompanying small one-bedroom apartments overhead, where the residents would live. The task had taken him months, demanding long hours and late nights. But when the activity stopped, he always ended up right where he started. Up to his ears in guilt.

Matthew wiped a large hand across his forehead. He had to move forward, to make amends somehow. To honor the man who had changed his life.

But how?

He fiddled with a thin strip of wood, rolling it between his fingers as he studied the partially completed landscape. This new kind of art that Mac invented could be the perfect way to continue his legacy. *If* he could figure out some way to put it out into the world, where it belonged.

It's hardly rocket science.

Penny's earlier words played over again in his mind. Hands-on skills were one thing, but if Matthew stood a chance of making Mac Conlin a household name, he was going to need some serious help in the marketing department. Too bad the only marketing executive he knew was also the one woman he had never been able to resist. The one with eyes the color of seafoam at high tide. The one with a heart of gold and the sweetest laugh he'd ever heard.

The one who left him behind.

Matthew dropped the wooden shard. Of course, the only logical solution would be to ask her for help. To be adult about the whole thing, leave the past where it belonged, and remain impartial. But Matthew wasn't sure if he could. He hadn't talked with Penny for more than five minutes, and he was already making all kinds of careless mistakes. Daydreaming about their past and wondering about her present. What would happen if they worked together?

Nope. Not going to happen.

Matthew couldn't let her get in his head. Or his heart. He couldn't—*wouldn't*—risk experiencing that kind of loss again. Letting her go had been bad enough the first time. And then, Mac…

Matthew set his jaw. No way was he about to let Penelope Shay hurt him again. Or even just distract him. This project was far too important, and his heart was still too raw. He had to stay focused. On something other than Penny.

"I'll figure this out, Mac," Matthew murmured, referring to much more than the thousand-piece jigsaw puzzle before him. "I promise, you won't be forgotten."

Chapter Two

The first things to greet Penny as she walked through the door of the Sweet Surprises Bakery the next morning were the comforting holiday scents of cinnamon, clove, and nutmeg. The delicious smell elicited an appreciative hum.

Something smells good.

The bakery looked good, too. As her gaze swept through the small space, Penny's chest swelled with sisterly pride. The bakery couldn't have possibly been a more accurate representation of her brother. Clean lines and a sleek matte black chandelier perfectly fit Andrew's modern aesthetic, but the antique tin ceiling tiles and the graying reclaimed wood running across the bottom of the glass-topped display counter gave a nod to the nostalgia that so often inspired him. The royal purple wainscoting on the otherwise pale gray walls lent a much-needed pop of color to the space while also complementing the front door, which sported the same lively hue. Through a large rectangular window in the wall behind the front counter, Penny could see Andrew already hard at work, whistling as he poured batter into two large sheet trays.

The sight gave her already frazzled nerves a jump start. Aside from a short weekend trip to attend his high-school graduation, Penny had been almost completely absent from Andrew's life here in Cedar Ridge. Things hadn't gotten much better after he left for college, choosing to attend a prestigious culinary school in Europe. While the siblings had kept in touch, their time together had been practically nonexistent. And now they were supposed to be working together?

Penny drew in a deep breath, vainly trying to expel her guilt at having abandoned her brother on the exhale.

Here goes nothing.

Passing through the swinging door that led to the back room, she called out a tentative greeting.

"Good morning."

"Pinkie!" Andrew's clear blue eyes sparkled when they spotted her.

Penny fought the urge to groan. Looks like Andrew hadn't forgotten his childhood nickname for her. Hopefully, he wasn't planning on reviving it long-term.

After setting the mixing bowl down on one of two large stainless-steel worktables, he gave his hands a quick wipe on his apron, then jogged over to envelop her in a huge bear hug.

"Ah, I've missed you!"

Penny laughed, allowing herself to relax as she returned his affectionate squeeze with one of her own. "I've missed you, too, Andrew."

As the two parted, tiny pinpricks stung her eyes. The reality of their situation was beginning to sink in.

"Hey, Andy?" she began.

"Yeah, Pinkie?"

"Thanks."

Confusion darkened his gaze as his brow furrowed, causing a lock of jet-black hair to slide over his eyes. "For what?"

Penny lifted her arms and gestured around the workroom. "For…this. It means a lot to me to be here."

Andrew raised both hands—and an eyebrow for good measure—while taking a step back in mock concern. "Whoa, hold on. You're not going to cry on me, are you?"

Penny rolled her eyes. It was just like her brother to shy away from an emotional response.

"Maybe," she teased. "I haven't decided yet."

"So I'm still in danger?" Andrew joked.

"Afraid so."

Andrew laughed, a free and easy sound at complete odds with Penny's apprehension.

He's making this seem so easy.

But her guilt at having left him wasn't going to go away that quickly.

"Well, in that case—" he grinned, rubbing his hands together in eager anticipation "—I'd say it's time to change the subject. Besides, I've been dying to fill you in on my master plan!"

Penny chuckled, amused by her brother's contagious enthusiasm. "I can't wait to hear all about it."

Andrew's slanted grin grew even wider as he reached into his apron's front pocket.

"Feast your eyes on this!"

Penny examined the poster in his hand, quickly understanding the source of his excitement.

"A state-wide Christmas-cookie contest?"

"Pretty cool, huh?" Andrew proclaimed, clearly satisfied with his find. "The winner gets featured in that travel magazine, *Eating America*. It's crazy popular. That has to help with publicity, right?"

"Andrew, this is great!" The wheels in Penny's head began to spin as she gladly shifted into work mode. Coming up with a steady stream of ideas had always been a welcome relief from fruitless worrying, and today was no exception. "Talk about launching the business with a bang."

"It gets better," Andrew said. "First place also wins a huge cash prize."

Penny froze in place. A cash prize? Large enough to buy Nana's house? Was this God's answer to last night's prayer?

"What do you need to do to qualify?" she asked, trying hard not to get her hopes up yet.

"Way ahead of you, sis," Andrew intoned, his chest puffing with pride. "I submitted my application two months ago, and yesterday was the qualifying round."

"And?" she persisted. "Did you get in?"

He leveled her with a disbelieving stare, then quipped, "Does Santa wear red?"

"Oh, Andrew, that's incredible!" Penny launched forward and gave her brother another hug. "I'm so proud of you!"

"Thanks." She heard the smile lurking behind his voice as Andrew returned her affection with a quick squeeze.

"This is exactly what we need," Penny mused aloud. But then she quickly amended, "To kick-start our social-media strategy, that is. People love a good story. Plus, the exposure will drive viewers to your bakery's website and increase sales, even before the contest."

"Ah," Andrew corrected, raising a finger in protest. "*Our* bakery."

"Right..." She faltered, only enjoying the gratitude welling up in her heart for just the briefest of moments before a familiar remorse rose to overshadow it. "Our bakery."

If she sounded unsure, Andrew didn't seem to notice. He simply pointed to a rolled-up purple apron on the worktable.

"Now, quit stalling and put your apron on—we've got a lot of work to do to prepare."

"Wait...*we*?" The word slammed into Penny like a fully loaded eighteen-wheeler. "Why we?"

"Every contestant needs a sous chef," Andrew replied, turning back to his sheets full of cake batter. "And I chose you."

"Me?" Penny choked out the word around the sizable lump in her throat.

"Yes, you," Andrew insisted, sliding the sheets into the oven, then closing the door. "You're my partner, aren't you?" He sent her a carefree grin as he set the large stainless-steel mixing bowl in the industrial sink.

Penny could only nod an affirmation. She had known when she'd agreed to partner with Andrew in the bakery that although her official role in the company was as bookkeeper and marketing specialist, she would also be helping in the kitchen. But as a contestant? In a state-wide cookie contest?

She leaned one hand on the counter while the other found a resting spot over her now-roiling stomach. On the outside, she was all right, but inside was all chaos and turmoil. Penny's heart thundered in her chest with the force and fury of a winter storm. Stainless-steel tables began to sway as lightheadedness set in.

Oh, this was *not* good.

"Hey, Pinkie," Andrew said, his brow furrowing in concern. "Are you feeling okay?"

"Fine," Penny stated, more emphatically than was strictly necessary. "I'm fine."

Though Andrew opted not to push, the curious look on his face told another story.

He couldn't have known, of course, that what he was proposing scared the living daylights out of her. How could he? Penny had worked long and hard to overcome her tendency toward introversion, and most days, she put up a brave front. But presenting a marketing strategy in front of a board of executives was nothing compared to a baking competition, especially in front of such a large audience.

No. She couldn't do this. There was no way!

But...this was her only chance to save their childhood home. Besides, making this bakery a success was Andrew's dream. She hadn't been there for him when he needed her. How could she leave him in the lurch again?

This was her chance to make things right.

Still, the rapid beating of her heart reminded Penny that a lot more was at stake than just a cookie competition. All that pressure. All those people. And a secret heart condition that was in serious danger of being aggravated by the stress.

What could possibly go wrong?

"This is worse than I thought."

Standing in the as-yet-unfinished unit, Matthew wracked his head searching for an acceptable explanation. He had known that his friend and business partner, Connor Wilkinson, had fallen behind on this project before he left town for a family emergency, but other than some roughed-in plumbing and drywall, this final Main Street shop looked as though it hadn't been touched in weeks.

He rubbed his forehead as a dull ache began to set in.

So much for working on Mac's project. This shop needed to be first priority if they stood a chance of having it ready for the grand opening.

"What's this unit supposed to be, anyway?" Cassandra, who was beside him, asked.

Slanting a glance in her direction, Matthew could practically see the gears turning in the newly minted interior designer's mind.

"A beauty salon." Matthew reached inside his jacket pocket and pulled out a folded stack of papers. "This is the design plan for the space."

Cassandra took the papers from his hand and gave them a quick once-over.

Matthew studied his sister as she worked. While Cassandra had been gifted with extraordinary creativity and an astute sense of style, she was also remarkably adept at maximizing a space's capacity for efficiency.

"Whose unit is this?" Cassandra asked.

"Morgan Thompson."

"Okay…" Cassandra nodded, deep in thought. "I can work with that."

Matthew remembered Morgan as being a member of the cheer squad that rallied the crowd during his football games.

She was also the reason for Penny's attendance. If she hadn't been supporting her best friend, Matthew figured the shy bookworm wouldn't have ever ventured out on a Friday night to sit by herself high up on the bleachers. Although as their friendship had progressed, he had hoped that her reason for coming to the games had something to do with him, too.

"Hello… Earth to Matthew."

Coming out of his reverie, he found Cassandra shaking her head, an amused expression on her face.

"Boy, you have got it *bad*."

Matthew resisted the urge to sigh. His sister never quit.

"What I've got," he returned, "is a problem. And you're here to help me solve it."

Instead of moving in the direction of his conversational pivot, Cassandra simply crossed her arms and stared him down.

"Fine, but before I do, you have to answer me one question."

Matthew clenched his jaw, already anticipating what that question would be and not liking it one bit.

"Do you still have feelings for Penny?"

To his sister's credit, she'd softened her typically confident tone and opted for a sympathetic approach. But Matthew was neither ready nor willing to answer her query.

The tinkling of bells and an accompanying draft of cold air signaled the arrival of a visitor.

Saved by the bells.

Overcome with a mixture of gratitude and relief, Matthew turned toward the door, and came face-to-face with the subject of their conversation.

"Penny?"

A thin line appeared between her eyebrows as she looked back and forth between Cassandra and Matthew. Her windswept hair was dusted with dozens of tiny snowflakes, and her cheeks were flushed pink, from the frigid winter air.

"Matthew?" It might have been the cold, or maybe his imagination, but her voice sounded a little breathless to his ears. "Hi. What are you doing here?"

"I work here," he replied. "Sort of."

It wasn't the most eloquent of explanations, but it didn't matter. Penny wasn't focused on him anymore. A sharp intake of breath told Matthew that she'd assessed the state of the unit and found it severely wanting.

"Oh, no," she whispered softly, her wide eyes darting between bare walls and concrete floors. "Morgan is going to freak out!"

"Not to worry," Cassandra said, stepping forward to calm her, as one would a frightened animal. "We can fix this. Right, Matt?"

"Hmm?" Matthew had been too busy counting snowflakes to follow. In response to his sister's incredulous glance, he cleared his throat and refocused. "Right."

"But we *do* have a problem with these designs," Cassandra stated bluntly, stepping closer to Penny and pointing at a spot on the papers. "The instructions aren't very clear, and the placement of these elements does nothing to maximize the space's potential."

Matthew closed the gap between them and joined the fray, trying desperately to keep his eyes on the designs and away from Penny's adorably furrowed brow. Soon, he noticed the soft scent of vanilla in the air, inviting him to lean in closer. He resisted, but just barely.

"The good news is, this is the last unit to be completed," Cassandra continued. "So we can focus our full attention on it."

"We?" Matthew dragged himself back to earth just in time to confront his sister. "Morgan hasn't hired you."

"Not *yet* she hasn't," Cassandra insisted. "But trust me, when she sees the ideas I have for this place, it'll be a done deal."

"Morgan's got a lot going on right now," Penny offered hesitantly. "I'm not sure she'd want to rethink her space."

"Then how about we do it for her?" Cassandra suggested, her eyes full of mischief. "You know her better than anyone, right? You can act as her stand-in, and the whole thing will be a big surprise."

Penny shifted, her discomfort clear. "I don't know…"

"At least let me show you what I'm thinking," Cassandra declared, rifling through her oversize tote to extract a large sketchpad. "Then you can decide."

His sister began pacing through the empty unit, her pencil flying across the page as she brought her ideas to life.

"You know," Matthew offered to Penny, leaning in a little closer than he really should have, "Cassandra may be a bit much, but she's also very talented. You don't have anything to worry about as far as her designs are concerned."

His sister's less-than-covert matchmaking, on the other hand, was an entirely different story.

Matthew felt his pulse kick up a notch when Penny flashed a grateful smile his way.

"Thanks, but it's not that," she replied softly. A shallow groove formed across her forehead as she shook her head. "Well, it's not *just* that."

"What's going on?" A swift mental kick soon followed his inquiry. He should be keeping his distance, not trying to play Prince Charming by coming to her rescue.

Penny's stormy blue-gray eyes were on him again, dejection lurking in their depths. "Andrew's roped me into a baking contest."

Matthew couldn't keep an amused grin from spreading across his face. "Rumpelstiltskin all over again, huh?"

In an instant, her expression changed, and the Penny he used to know appeared.

"Don't you dare," she warned, barely managing to hold back her laughter.

"Why not?" he asked, all too eager to hear that melodious laugh of hers again. "You passed, didn't you?"

Their gazes held for just a moment longer before the two burst into uncontrollable laughter.

Part of their sophomore English grade had required Penny and Matthew to act in the school's production of *Romeo and Juliet*. But even though she'd only had a small part, Penny had been so terrified of getting up on stage that she'd nearly fainted during dress rehearsal...twice. To save the play from disaster, their teacher eventually had pity on the poor girl and allowed her to complete a make-up assignment by entertaining kindergarteners during their library time.

Not that acting out a fairy tale as a one-woman show had been any easier for her. But while the assignment had been a crushing blow for Penny, it had been a golden opportunity for her secret admirer. Matthew had stepped in to help her prepare, and she had actually gone through with it. Kind of.

"I don't know what I would have done without your last-minute improv," Penny said, complimenting him as she wiped a few errant tears from her eyes. "I completely blanked!"

"Look on the bright side," Matthew said grinning as he parroted his words from so many years ago, "at least you didn't faint."

Penny released a sweet little chuckle before sobering again.

"That's more than I can say about this contest. I really don't know what I'm going to do. But I can't let Andrew down."

"Yeah." Matthew gave a quick nod. "I know what that's like."

Penny's inquisitive gaze flicked up to capture his, unspoken questions swimming in her eyes.

He shouldn't. He knew he shouldn't. He wouldn't go there. But, man, did she ever make it hard for him to keep quiet.

An exaggerated sigh drew their attention to Cassandra, who had long since completed her sketch.

"Comments from the peanut gallery?" Matthew quipped, trying and failing to squelch the uneasy feeling that settled in the pit of his stomach at her approach. Cassandra was up to something. That was never good.

"Isn't it obvious?" she remarked, completely ignoring the pleading look he sent her way. "You both have a problem the other can solve. So work together!"

"Oh, no," Penny said, raising her hands in defense. "We couldn't."

Whatever Matthew's problem was, she was *not* about to become his solution. It was way too dangerous for her heart, both physically and emotionally.

"Why not?" Cassandra asked, undaunted, once more reaching into her purse. "You clearly make a great team."

"That was a long time ago," Matthew pointed out, but his sister was too focused on swiping through pictures on her cell phone to care.

"Here." She thrust the phone toward Penny. "What do you think?"

The object in question was a large mural. The scene, a desert sunset, seemed to be made entirely out of thin strips of wood running in horizontal lines across the frame, stained in varying hues ranging from vibrant reds to deep browns.

"Cassandra, this is amazing!" Penny said, gushing. "Where did you find this?"

"Matt made it." She grinned wide.

"You made that?" Penny asked as she marveled at the

image. She turned and found a suddenly self-conscious Matthew looking down at the floor.

"Yep."

"Matthew, it's gorgeous!" Penny knew that she was treading on thin ice, but if the soft spot she carried in her heart for the unexpected artist hadn't gotten the better of her, Penny's admiration for his innovative artwork certainly would have. "I've never seen anything like it—not even in New York!"

Matthew seemed to tense at that comment. "So you became an art connoisseur in your time away?"

His words didn't *sound* antagonistic, but at the same time, Matthew hardly seemed pleased by the idea. If he was, the frown tugging at his ruggedly handsome features strongly indicated otherwise.

"Oh, yeah," Penny joked, deciding that a lighter mood was in order. "In New York, museum-hopping is practically a sport."

Though his eyes remained fixed on the ground, a slight smile played at his mouth and set her heart to fluttering.

Foolish girl. She should be making her escape, not cracking jokes.

"Matthew runs a contracting business," Cassandra explained, jumping in to get their conversation back on track. "He's managed all the renovations that have been taking place in Cedar Ridge."

"Where does your art fit into the business?" Penny asked, still addressing the brooding contractor.

"It doesn't." Matthew shrugged, crossing muscular arms over his broad chest. "At least, not yet."

"You mean you don't sell it?" She gaped. "Why?"

"I work with my hands, not computers," Matthew hedged. "If I wanted to showcase the murals—which I do, eventually—I'd need a website and social media and all kinds of other things that I know nothing about." When he finally cast a wary glance her way, Penny could see that his eyes had clouded over, darkening to a rich emerald. "I'm trying, but it's a steep learning curve."

Oh, why did he have to send that soulful glance her way? Didn't he know how much he still affected her?

"I know it seems daunting, but it's really not that hard." Penny hoped her encouraging smile would open him up. It did not. "I could—"

Penny practically bit her tongue to stop herself. What had happened to her resolve? She had almost offered to help him. Spending even more time with the ridiculously handsome man was *exactly* what she should *not* be doing.

"Help?" Cassandra interjected, finishing Penny's deliberately unfinished sentence. "I thought as much."

"I'm sure Penny has other things to do." Matthew's stare would have been positively withering had it been directed at anyone other than Cassandra. Instead of stopping her, somehow, it only seemed to energize her.

"Like prepare for a contest?" she quizzed, unaffected in the least by his firm warning. "Sounds pretty serendipitous to me."

"I don't think that's a good idea," Penny offered, knowing full well that her tentative protest would be helpless to stop Cassandra's efforts.

"Why not?"

"Because..."

What reason *could* Penny give for not wanting to work with Matthew? She couldn't tell the truth—not without alerting the entire town to her heart condition, anyway.

But besides that, Cassandra *did* have a point. If it hadn't been for Matthew, she never would have managed to get through that English assignment on her own. He had bolstered her confidence, encouraged her, and practiced with her more times than she could count. He had cared. And that had made her want to move past her fears.

For him.

A cold wave of trepidation washed over her at the thought. If she agreed to this, they'd go from tiptoeing on ice to playing with fire, and after what she had just gone through, Penny wasn't ready to get burned again. The last thing she needed was another heartache, literally or metaphorically.

"I'm not hearing a good reason," Cassandra said, prodding her. "In fact, I'm not hearing *any* reason."

"Maybe we both have reasons we'd prefer to keep to ourselves," Matthew interrupted.

Penny turned toward him, wondering about his cryptic comment, but Matthew's focus was on his sister.

What was *his* reason for avoiding her? Was he upset with her for leaving, too?

An embarrassed flush crept up her neck at the memory, but it quickly turned into indignation. This was ridiculous! Cassandra was absolutely right. Regardless of their past, she and Matthew were both adults, and they both had need of each other's talents. Enough of this! It was time to take charge.

"Maybe we could both shelve those reasons for the time being."

Two pairs of eyes suddenly jerked toward her—one showed excitement, the other, reserve.

"I mean, it would only be for a few weeks," Penny continued. "What's the point of struggling on our own? We need each other."

Two pairs of eyes suddenly widened.

"I mean, we need each other's *help*," Penny quickly added. "What do you say, Matthew? Your contest training in exchange for my marketing strategy. Do we have a deal?"

Matthew eyed her warily, but despite his guarded demeanor, there was a strange sort of softness in his eyes.

Was that hope hiding somewhere behind his protests? Did it really matter?

She was spared the agony of mulling over those questions when Matthew, having made his decision, gave a curt nod and extended his hand.

"Okay," he simply said.

Penny hesitated for just a moment before slipping her hand into his. The sudden rush of warmth that resulted took her by surprise, drawing her gaze to their hands.

Hold it together, girl!

Because if she didn't, she'd end up falling for him—fast.

Drawing in a quick breath, Penny steeled herself as best she could. She would not let Matthew Banks distract her. No matter how attractive he happened to be. This was a business arrangement, nothing more.

Now, if only she could convince her heart.

Chapter Three

"I'm *so* excited to be working on Morgan's unit," Cassandra said enthusiastically as she walked arm in arm with Penny along Cedar Ridge's picturesque Main Street. Before sharing her ideas for Morgan's space, Cassandra had insisted on a walking tour en route to the coffee shop owned by David Harrison.

Beside her, Matthew shook his head. "You say that about all your clients."

"And I mean it every time."

As they walked along the town's main strip, Penny marveled at the amount of work that had gone into the revitalization effort. Along Main Street, an array of colorful doors accented the cream-colored storefronts, recently renovated for use by the returning residents. Sleek monochrome awnings boasted the names of their respective shops, lending a unified feel to the strip. Oversize wreaths wrapped in bright red ribbons adorned the lampposts that lined either side of the street, and lights had been strung across the road in a zigzag pattern that was sure to wow come nightfall. In the center of it all, a large banner reading Merry Christmas from Cedar Ridge! hung grandly across the road.

"Take a look in here." Cassandra guided Penny to a large window. The two pressed their hands to the glass as they took a peek inside. "This is going to be a craft supply shop."

"Wow," Penny said, taking in the simple, yet cozy space. "It's beautiful."

"This place belongs to Bridget Davies," Cassandra informed her, turning away from the window and resuming their brisk pace. She confided to Penny, "She was my guinea pig. Her shop was my first big project."

"Poor, brave girl," Matthew teased, to which Cassandra responded with a good-natured poke into his ribs.

"Watch it," she warned, her sly smile undermining the threat.

"How is Bridget doing?" Penny asked, willing herself to stay focused on Cassandra and not her attractive younger brother.

"Oh, are you two close?" Cassandra asked.

"Not really," Penny admitted. "But Bridget was good friends with my brother, Andrew."

Bridget had also harbored a massive crush on the woefully oblivious Andrew, but Penny thought it best to keep that kind of information to herself.

Soon they reached their destination. Cassandra pulled open a heavy-looking wooden door with an antique leaded-glass insert and ushered Penny inside, where the fragrant scent of freshly brewed coffee wrapped itself around her like a warm hug.

"Hello," Cassandra called out as she and Matthew joined Penny in the warmth of the shop.

Penny nearly jumped out of her coat when a curly mass of unruly black hair sprung up from behind a dark wooden countertop.

"Hey Cassandra!" David called out in greeting. "Back so soon?"

"It's your own fault," Cassandra chided as she strode up to the counter. "Whatever you put in those lattes of yours has got me hooked. I can't seem to go a day without one." She turned and aimed a wink in Penny's direction. "Or two."

"That's music to my ears," he grinned. "So that's one latte for you." David paused, pushing a pair of heavy, clear-rimmed glasses higher on his nose. "And how about you two?" he asked, his dark brown eyes bouncing back and forth from Penny to Matthew.

"Do you have peppermint mocha on the menu?" Penny asked the charismatic barista. "It feels like ages since I've had one."

"That sounds good," Matthew affirmed behind her. "Make it two."

"Oh, but make mine a decaf, please," Penny interjected, belatedly remembering that she was on strict orders to limit her caffeine intake.

"Can do," David replied, turning to grab a couple of tins off the dark floating shelves above the counter. "Just give me a couple of minutes to get your drinks ready."

"Take your time," Cassandra said, making her way to a round glass-topped table situated near the large storefront window. "We're planning to stay a while today."

Penny followed her lead, shedding her jacket before taking a seat.

"So what do you think?" Cassandra asked once they had gotten settled. "About the design, I mean."

For the first time since setting foot inside the café, Penny allowed her gaze to roam about the space. The walls, painted a neutral tan, served as the perfect foil for the vibrant burgundy accent wall behind the counter. Black floating shelves positioned above David's workspace displayed an assortment of canisters in varying shapes and sizes. The exposed rafters were also painted black, and gave the café a modern vibe, but the aged wooden counter and gas fireplace kept it from feeling too stark. Smooth jazz played softly throughout, inviting customers to linger without overwhelming conversations.

"I really like it," Penny said. "It seems to suit David perfectly."

Much like the aesthetic in the Sweet Surprises Bakery...

"Wait a minute," she began. "Did you design the interior of the bakery, too?"

Cassandra grinned. "Guilty as charged."

"In that case, I'd say that Morgan's salon is in good hands."

Cassandra's dark eyes gleamed as she pulled her sketchpad and pencil from her large tote. "Has Morgan changed much since high school?"

"Not at all," Penny said.

"Excellent." Cassandra's head dipped down as she made a quick note on the page. "In that case, the accent color is going to be teal."

David walked over, setting a frothy cup of coffee down in front of Penny. Wasting no time at all, she raised the large white mug and took a sip of the rich, flavorful brew.

"Mmm..." she hummed, closing her eyes as the tastes of dark chocolate and fresh peppermint mingled in her mouth. "I could get used to this."

"Thank you," David chuckled. "That's quite the compliment."

When Penny opened her eyes, she was surprised to find Matthew watching her. He averted his gaze quickly enough, but it hadn't been fast enough to hide the melancholy note lingering in the depths of those emerald eyes.

A note he clearly hadn't wanted her to see.

Out of nowhere, a sharp pain sliced through her chest, stealing the air from her lungs.

Not now...

"Penny?" Cassandra's concern quickly brought Penny back to reality. "Are you feeling all right?"

"Fine," she lied, working hard to keep up the appearance of normalcy.

"Are you sure?" Cassandra frowned. "You look a little flushed."

"Oh, yeah." Penny waved a hand in practiced nonchalance. "I'm just a little warm in here." She hoped her easy smile would placate the intuitive designer, but she still seemed unsure. "Guess I'll think twice about wearing a turtleneck from now on."

"I can turn down the heat," David offered, already on his way to the thermostat before Penny had the chance to protest.

"And I'll open a window," Cassandra insisted.

"Oh, you don't—" Penny tried to protest, but it was no use. Clearly, small-town hospitality was still alive and well.

"You sure you're okay?" Penny turned to find Matthew leaning forward in his seat, regarding her with soft eyes.

"I'm good," she said, much more confidently than she felt. *For now, anyway.*

"If you say so," he said, seeming unconvinced.

"Better?" Cassandra asked as she returned to her seat.

"Yes, thank you." Penny sent a sincere smile her way. "I'm more than ready to look at those designs now."

"Me, too," Matthew agreed, sliding the sketchbook in his direction. "But Cass, you are aware that the grand opening is less than three weeks away, right?" he pointed out. "Are we going to have time to finish this if we start from scratch?"

Cassandra sent an unimpressed glance his way. "I'm sorry, are we not starting from scratch right now?"

Matthew nodded through a grimace. "Fair point."

"But, yes, we most certainly will," she asserted confidently. "*If* we all pitch in."

She slid a pointed glance at Penny then.

"That shouldn't be a problem," Penny answered.

As long as there wasn't any heavy lifting involved, anyway...

"Great!" Cassandra reached for her sketchbook and hunched over her creation in eager anticipation. "Let's talk design."

As Cassandra began to outline in detail the plans she had for the salon, simultaneously adding to the drawing and making winding to-do lists all the while, Penny felt her nerves begin to recede.

Morgan will definitely approve.

Matthew drew in a deep breath as he stepped out of Morgan's shop and into the fresh air the following afternoon. It had been a long day, and he was beat. Unsurprisingly, Penny loved Cassandra's designs, and once his sister had gotten the go-ahead, she wasted no time in ordering the required materials. There was still a lot of work to be done, and the time frame would be tight, especially with Connor gone, but barring any unexpected setbacks, Matthew figured they would have the place finished just in time.

Strolling along Main Street, he couldn't believe how much had changed in the last few months. He and Connor had been working hard to make sure that things were up and running in time for the grand opening, but now, the end was in sight.

Finally.

Once this last unit was finished, Matthew was taking some time off.

He scoffed, remembering the reason he'd been pushing himself so hard in the first place. Would he even be able to relax for long enough to enjoy a vacation? Maybe after implementing his plan to honor Mac, but not a moment before.

But really, even if Matthew did decide to take off, it wasn't like there was anywhere for him to go. Visiting his parents had been out of the question ever since his father had taken to pretending like he didn't exist. It beat arguing by a long shot, but it still stung to know that he wasn't welcome around his own father.

Garrett Banks was a demanding man. He could be downright overbearing at times, and none more so than when Matthew had decided to quit college. The two had gotten into several heated arguments, each one successively worse than the last, before Matthew ultimately went against his father's wishes and withdrew. Things hadn't been the same between them since.

Matthew knew that deep down, his father meant well, but he'd also been unyielding in his refusal to consider things from Matthew's perspective. At the time, Garrett Banks hadn't been ready to accept the fact that he didn't know what was best for his son. And now...well, Matthew figured his silence said it all.

What a stark contrast to Mac. He had accepted Matthew just the way he was, taking him in without asking questions. He didn't expect anything other than the manual labor he'd been promised. As a result, Matthew had finally felt free to simply be himself. And what a relief it had been to find that for once, who he was had been enough.

No. More than enough.

Matthew gave his head a quick jerk as his chest squeezed to the point of discomfort. It had been almost a year since Mac left for that fateful delivery last winter, but it seemed as if Matthew was feeling his absence even more acutely these days. Maybe it was because the anniversary of the accident was fast approaching. Or maybe it was because of this deal he'd inadvertently made with Penny. Or, most likely, the guilt he'd been carrying around since last year was finally starting to wear him down. Either way, he knew that things couldn't continue this way for much longer. Matthew had spent the better part of a year trying to outrun his remorse. It hadn't worked thus far.

Stepping down off the sidewalk, Matthew cast a quick glance in either direction before crossing over to the other side of Main Street. He needn't have bothered. Traffic was always light around town. Hopefully that would change soon.

He cleared the steps up to the covered walkway in front

of Sweet Surprises in one long stride, stopping short as he caught sight of himself in the window. Stray plaster dusted his jeans as if from a recent snowfall. He brushed it off before rubbing away some dirt from his cheek. And was that sawdust in his hair?

Yikes. Speaking of hair, his was an absolute mess. Flattened in spots and sticking up at odd angles in others. The hazards of wearing a hard hat. Matthew ran one hand through the flattened mass, then tried his best to tame the offending locks into a halfway decent style. Today was his first day on the job—as Penny's coach, that is. He probably should have thought to clean up a little beforehand.

Matthew's hands stilled as cold reality washed over him like an icy snowdrift.

He was preening for Penny.

Oh, man, this was not good. They weren't even one day into their training and already he was acting like a lovesick teenager.

Clearly, this arrangement was going to be a lot harder than he thought.

Er, hoped.

He still couldn't believe that Penny had gone along with Cassandra's ridiculous idea. To say that it had surprised him would be a severe understatement, especially given how skittish she had been initially. But once she agreed to the exchange—and looked at him with those beautiful blue eyes of hers—how could he refuse?

Matthew pushed out a heavy breath.

He couldn't. That was exactly the problem.

Forcing himself to quit while he was behind, Matthew sidestepped toward the front door and entered the bakery.

Let's just get this over with.

The sooner they completed their deal, after all, the sooner he could get back to safeguarding his heart.

At first, he didn't see anyone. Then he noticed Penny through a window behind the counter. She was sitting at a stainless-steel table, her gaze low. It wasn't until he'd made it to the swinging door that led to the back workroom, however, that he realized she was praying.

Hands clasped tight, eyes closed, brow furrowed... Yup, there was no doubt about it. Penny's lips were moving almost imperceptibly as she poured out her heart before God. But her expression gave him pause. It wasn't the serene look of a woman resting in the Lord, but rather one fervently petitioning for something.

What was going on with her?

Not that it was any of his business, he quickly reminded himself. Still, the scene stopped him in his tracks. It wasn't as if he could barge into the kitchen now that he knew she was praying.

He stood by the door for several moments before wondering if this qualified as being creepy. Definitely not the impression that he was going for. But Matthew didn't want to disturb her, either. Slowly, he pushed open the door, stepping through as quietly as possible.

Despite his best efforts, Penny heard the noise. Instantly, her head shot up and her eyes were on him again.

"Matthew." She smiled, but it seemed forced. Was she upset that he'd walked in on her?

"I, uh, I'm sorry if I interrupted you," he mumbled, suddenly feeling as awkward as a kid talking to his first crush.

"That's all right." She waved the thought away with those melancholy-laden words, evading his gaze all the while. Then she stood slowly, revealing a long-sleeved, sage-green jersey dress that ended at the top of her knee-high boots. "I was just about finished, anyway."

Matthew's heart did an unexpected somersault at the sight. Had she remembered that his favorite color was green?

Quickly, he clenched his jaw, bracing against the foolish hope that sprung to life with reckless abandon.

Did it matter?

He knew it shouldn't. Not if he wanted to keep his heart intact. So why was he suddenly feeling so frustrated?

"Can I take your jacket?"

When Penny looked his way, every trace of her earlier vulnerability was gone, replaced by a polite professionalism that bothered Matthew more than he cared to admit.

What happened to the sweet, shy girl he used to know? The one that stammered and blushed and wore her heart on her sleeve?

"Sure, thanks."

He shrugged out of the jacket in question and handed it to Penny, their hands touching briefly as he did. Penny ducked her head, but the gesture couldn't conceal the pretty blush blossoming on her cheeks.

Maybe that girl was still in there?

Matthew ran a hand through his hair. It would be better for him if she wasn't. It was going to be hard enough keeping his distance from Penny without her reminding him of all the reasons why he'd once fallen head over heels for her.

"Thanks for meeting with me after hours," Penny began as she hung his jacket in a minuscule closet.

"No sweat," he replied. "I get it. In a town this small, the less people know, the better."

"Ri-i-ight." The word came out slowly, as though she had only just now considered that idea. "But really, the only person I'm concerned about is Andrew."

"Andrew?" Matthew repeated, surprised. "He doesn't know about this?"

"No," Penny admitted through twisted lips. Then, in a smaller voice, she added, "He has no idea how scared I am."

How could those barely whispered words tug so strongly at

his heart? And how could he not want to jump in and save her in response? To protect her from everything that was causing her pain? To be her knight in shining armor?

Matthew squeezed his hands into fists. No, he couldn't do that. But the thought was tempting.

"And I don't want him to find out," she went on, determination underscoring her words.

"I won't say a word," Matthew promised.

"Great. I wasn't sure what you had in mind as far as training goes," Penny began, words measured, gaze low. "So I took out some equipment, just in case."

She gestured to the worktable, populated with mixing bowls of varying sizes, an assortment of ingredients, and a large stand mixer.

"The contest requires us to make and decorate several different types of cookies within a short time frame," she explained, her voice sounding far too even to his ears. "We won't know what the theme will be until the day of the contest, but we do know there will be a structural component involved."

"So you'll be building something," Matthew clarified.

"Yes, some kind of three-dimensional Christmas display."

"Well, I'll definitely be able to help with that," Matthew confirmed. "These days, I practically eat, sleep, and breathe construction."

Penny turned toward him, smiling sweetly. "Yes, and I can see that you've been hard at work."

She gestured to a spot on his shirt, and he looked down to find even more dried plaster.

Great.

"Sorry." Matthew swiped at the mark until it rubbed off. "I did a quick cleanup before coming over, but my jacket was on."

"Don't apologize." Penny seemed to relax in response to his sheepish explanation. "It's just part of the job. I can't tell you how many times I've ended up with flour on my clothes or icing in my hair."

Matthew chucked at the thought. "Now that I'd like to see."

Not that it would be wise. On the contrary, it would be pure torture to see her so adorably disheveled without being able to do a thing about it.

"You might." Penny's gaze ran the length of the table, as she seemed to be considering their options. "Depending on what you have in store."

Penny's gaze searched him out as if on instinct. She didn't say a word, but the slight pinch in her nose told him everything he needed to know.

She was remembering their high school partnership, just like he was.

"I suppose we should start with a baseline," he suggested, being very careful to remain impartial and to keep both his mind and this conversation in the present. "See what we're working with."

"And…how do you propose we do that?" she asked, more warily than he'd prefer.

He understood her hesitation completely. That didn't mean he liked it.

"Set you up for a trial run and see how you do."

His answer came out more flatly than he'd intended, chasing the light from her eyes.

"Oh."

Was she…disappointed? Matthew could not figure this woman out.

"Um, yeah, that's fine," Penny continued, tucking a strand of silky brown hair behind her ear. It wasn't lost on him that her hand was shaking as she did so.

Matthew cleared his throat as he stepped back, opting to take a cautious approach by putting some distance between them.

"Okay," he announced, more to himself than to Penny. "Enough talk. Let's get you ready."

"So let me get this straight. You're training, for a cookie competition...with Matthew Banks?" Perfectly shaped eyebrows drew together over Morgan's green eyes. "Does not compute."

Penny's internal alarm bells began to ring at her friend's lackluster response. The Morgan she knew would have cheered at the revelation. She might have even thrown in a victory dance for good measure. The one staring back through her phone's screen did no such thing.

As if sensing Penny's concern, Morgan slanted her head and smiled. That might have fooled someone else, but Penny knew better.

"Girl, how in the world did you pull that one off?"

Penny released a gentle laugh. It may just be for show, but it was still nice to hear something that more closely resembled Morgan pre-Brendan.

"The Little Miss Matchmakers strike again," Penny offered, shrugging her hands up at her sides. "Cassandra's an extremely difficult person to say no to."

Morgan scoffed. "Maybe I should fly her out for the weekend." Immediately, she cringed. "Sorry, didn't mean to get negative."

Penny's earlier concerns were confirmed. Morgan was an eternal optimist. Something was definitely wrong.

"That's okay," Penny said "Want to tell me what's going on?"

Her best friend hesitated, tilting her head forward and sending her shoulder-length auburn hair cascading down in gentle waves.

"Is it the move?" Penny persisted. "Or Brendan?"

Morgan dropped her gaze. "Partly." Then after a moment,

she added, "Mostly." She heaved a tired sigh. "I just don't know what to think."

Before Penny could respond, Morgan had pushed her hair back and was sitting upright once more.

Time's up.

Despite the outward show of bravado, however, her gaze still avoided the camera. "Enough about me. Tell me more about this deal."

"It's okay, Morgan," Penny reassured her. "I'm always here for you."

"I know," Morgan replied. "But I want to hear about you, too. I mean, this is pretty huge." Finally, her eyes were back on Penny. "How do you feel about working with your high-school crush?"

Now, it was Penny's turn to sigh. "Honestly… I feel conflicted."

To Penny's delight, the smile that blossomed actually reached Morgan's eyes, where it quickly morphed into mischief.

"Is he still your dream guy?"

Penny's heart jumped to attention, reminding her of why she couldn't afford to go down that road again.

"I don't think he can be."

Morgan's lips dipped low. "Why not?"

Because it would be irresponsible—not to mention terrifying—to start a relationship in this condition, that's why.

Penny wished she could be honest with Morgan—so much so that it felt like a heavy weight was pressing upon her chest, willing her to share. She had to admit, it would be nice to have at least one person to confide in. But Nick's rejection was still too raw. How would Morgan respond? How would anyone respond, for that matter? Penny didn't know, but this was a chance she wasn't yet willing to take. Keeping her illness a secret was better for everyone.

"Matthew seems kind of guarded," Penny offered instead.

"Well, sometimes." She shook her head in correction. "I don't know, but I doubt he's still interested in me. High school was a long time ago."

"Love doesn't tell time."

Morgan's snappy quip caused an unexpected gurgle of laughter to bubble up in Penny.

"Where did you hear that one?" she asked.

"Same place I hear all of them." Morgan shrugged, her sly smirk hinting at the joke to come. "I made it up."

Penny's single gurgle was quickly followed by several giggles, and soon, both girls were chuckling.

At least Morgan's sense of humor was still intact. Maybe things weren't really as bad as they seemed.

"You know, you never did tell me," Morgan began once their laughter subsided. "How did you and Matthew leave off? You know, before your big move?"

Penny started squirming in her seat.

"I…" Penny hesitated. "I never told him."

"You *what*?" Morgan's eyebrows shot high above her widened eyes. "Penny! You mean you just left him there without any explanation?"

An all-too familiar heat began to rise, warming her cheeks.

"Oh, my, that explains so much," Morgan went on. "But why the secrecy? I thought you two liked each other."

"We did," Penny insisted. "But after Mom died, things got kind of awkward." Penny felt a stab of remorse at the memory. "I may or may not have pushed him away out of self-preservation."

On her first day back to school, Penny had just been trying to keep it together. *Fragile* wasn't a strong enough word to describe how broken up she'd felt inside. She had managed for a little while, but only until Matthew caught up to her between classes. All it took was one glimpse of the concern in his eyes to weaken her resolve. Pair that with the softness in his voice, and she'd been ready to cave. A very small part of her felt indignant over being on the receiving end of more pity, but mostly, Penny wanted nothing more than to seek solace in Matthew's arms.

And that had scared her to death.

"When he tried to talk to me, I was in such a bad headspace that I just brushed him off and ran away," she admitted softly. "I wasn't sure how to bounce back after that, so I just avoided him. Then Uncle Everett reached out. I thought it would be better for everyone if I just disappeared for a while."

And then, a while had turned into forever, which had ended much sooner than she thought it would.

"Yeah, I get what that's like," Morgan responded quietly.

Penny wondered what her friend meant by that. Maybe she had similar reasons for becoming a returning resident.

"I was really stupid," Penny confessed, looking down into her lap. "And so embarrassed. I was always just about to cry, and I never knew when that awful sadness would overtake me. Honestly, I just wanted to hide." She fiddled with a loose thread on her sweater. "But still, it did kind of hurt that Matthew kept his distance after that. I always wondered if he was just giving me the space I needed or if I had completely ruined things."

"Matthew is one of the good guys," Morgan said. "I'd be really surprised if he took offense at something like that."

"I think you may be right," Penny agreed. "But me leaving town without saying goodbye?"

"Yeah…" Morgan's lips twisted in thought. "That might be a bit problematic."

A cheerful chorus of bells sounded then, eliciting a scowl from Morgan.

"Ugh, break time's over," Morgan announced, tapping her screen to silence the alarm. "And way too quickly." She sighed.

"I have to go. But thanks for the chat. I really needed it."

"You know I'm always here for you," Penny insisted, now more curious than ever.

"I know." Morgan flashed a grateful smile. It wasn't her usual megawatt grin, but it was certainly better than nothing. "Love you, sis."

The affectionate endearment calmed Penny's racing thoughts. She and Morgan were more than friends—they were family. Honorary sisters. Penny could trust that whatever was going on with her, Morgan would tell her when the time was right. After all, wasn't she doing the exact same thing? Penny had no right to judge when it came to keeping secrets these days.

Even so, a pinch of guilt gave her pause. If she was so concerned about whatever Morgan was going through, wouldn't Morgan feel the same way about her? Maybe Penny should tell Morgan about her heart condition. Surely, she would understand. But would it be too much? Especially with everything else that she was dealing with?

"I love you, too, sis," Penny replied.

And she did. Far too much to share.

Chapter Four

"Nana, I'm home!" Penny called out as she stepped through the door the next day, stomping her shoes on the welcome mat to rid them of excess snow.

"Hi, honey!"

Betty Nesbitt's voice rang out from the kitchen, barely audible over the upbeat Christmas music that was blasting through a nearby stereo. A quick sniff confirmed Penny's suspicions—Nana was baking a batch of her famous gingerbread cookies. This week's family dinner was going to have a delicious ending.

Nana's gingerbread was unlike any that Penny had ever tasted. She claimed to use a secret ingredient in her batter, but she was so tight-lipped about the ingredient that not even Andrew was privy to it.

Penny hung her jacket and purse on the coatrack tucked neatly into the corner of the foyer, opting to wait for her brother to arrive before heading to the kitchen. Turning her attention to the impressive collection of family photos hanging in the hallway, Penny stopped short as a familiar scene caught her eye.

Andrew, not yet four, was fiddling with a floppy chef's hat that was several sizes too big for his head. Penny, proudly wearing a frilly pink apron, was intently stirring the contents of a bowl with a wooden spoon, lips pressed together around her tongue, which stuck out at an odd angle as she struggled to manipulate the batter. Between them, their mother was crouched down, one hand on either of her children's shoulders as she smiled into the camera with joy.

A smile played at the corners of Penny's lips, but it was frayed. How had her mother remained so joyful, even after her husband's passing?

Penny and Andrew's father had died suddenly when the children were still very young. Stomach cancer, undiagnosed for years, had gotten the better of him. The loss had shaken her mother badly, but she had remained strong, determined to be positive for her kids' sakes. Moving into Nana's colonial had made it easier for all of them to heal, marking a fresh start for the Shay family.

At least, until her Mom's heart condition flared up...

"Hey, Pinkie." Andrew's entrance broke into her thoughts, bringing her back to the present. Penny turned to find him taking his coat off behind her. Pausing, he took a deep breath. "Mmm, smells like somebody's been baking...without us!"

"You know Nana," Penny smiled. "Nothing's going to separate her from that secret recipe."

"Yeah, not even her grandkids," Andrew remarked. "But..." He lowered his voice to a conspiratorial whisper as he drew close. "What she doesn't know is, this is the year we're going to solve the mystery."

Penny's eyes narrowed in mock suspicion. "You don't mean..."

"Oh, yes, I do." Andrew's icy eyes shone with mischief. "We're going to figure out Nana's secret ingredient."

Penny chuckled. "I guess we're still better at being partners in crime than in business."

Andrew scoffed. "The two go hand in hand, at least in this case."

"So what's the game plan?" she asked, her question an implicit acceptance to Andrew's shenanigans. "We've already tried flattery, bribery, and begging, and nothing's worked so far."

Andrew waved a hand in dismissal of their previous failures. "Forget all that. Now that you're home, we're going to experiment and figure out the recipe for ourselves."

Penny raised an eyebrow at her overly ambitious younger brother. That sounded much more like a goal than a plan. "What makes you think it'll be so easy?"

"I didn't say it would be easy," Andrew pointed out. "Only that it's possible. And if we can pull it off, we're sure to win that contest."

"Right," Penny agreed, her trademark caution rising to up to rein in his zeal. "But if we don't, we'll have wasted valuable time that could have been better spent tweaking the recipes we do have."

"Excuse me?" Andrew said, feigning offense. "The recipes we've got are the result of years' worth of tweaking. They're as good as they're going to get!"

"Then why add Nana's gingerbread to the mix?" Penny asked. "Knowing her, the secret ingredient is going to be something completely unexpected."

"Exactly!" Andrew practically pounced on her description. "If we bake good cookies, we'll stand a chance of winning. But if we show the judges something they've never seen before…"

Penny hummed, deep in thought. He had her there. And if she stood a chance of saving their childhood home, they *had* to win this contest. But between her covert training and Matthew's marketing plan, there was still so much to do. So much that Andrew didn't know about.

The weight was back and pressing down upon her shoulders like an overstuffed backpack. Secret-keeping was turning out to be more costly than she'd thought it would be.

"Come on, Pinkie, let's blow these judges away with the

best gingerbread they've ever tasted," Andrew insisted. "What do you say?"

Penny held his gaze for as long as she could without caving. But ultimately, Andrew won out. He always did.

"All right," she said and nodded, with more enthusiasm than she felt. "Let's do this."

"Awesome!" Andrew's excitement was as palpable as it was infectious. "First things first—we need to get our hands on one of those gingerbread men. And I know just the way to do it."

"Good cop, bad cop?"

"Just like old times."

Then Andrew strode into the kitchen, announcing his arrival.

"What are you up to in here, Nana?" he asked cheerily.

If the scent of ginger and the garishly loud Christmas music weren't enough of an indication, her grandmother's posture, hunched over the oven and eyeing the cookies through the glass panel, would have provided the answer.

"The usual," Nana practically shouted over the music as she straightened to her full five feet. As she considered her grandchildren, a contagious spark of life darted about in her crystal-clear blue eyes. "I've just whipped up a double batch of my top-secret gingerbread recipe. Along with dinner, of course."

"Wow," Penny said enthusiastically. "It sounds like you've been busy."

"It's that time of year again." Betty absentmindedly swiped away a stray lock of silver hair that had escaped from the messy bun atop her head, then walked over to the speaker and lowered the volume. "So much to do, so little time."

"If only you had two able-bodied and willing grandchildren who could help you with all this baking," Andrew said.

Betty wagged her finger at her grandson, a kind smile tempering the reprimand. "Oh, no, you don't. I know what you're up to, Andrew, and it's not going to work."

"Aww, come on, Nana." Andrew sulked, throwing himself into character with his typical reckless abandon. "We'll keep it to ourselves—we promise."

"Now, Andrew, we've been through this a hundred times," Penny chimed in, slipping into her role with ease. "You heard Nana. If she doesn't want to tell us her recipe, then we shouldn't bother her about it."

"Speak for yourself, Pinkie," Andrew retorted. "It's a family secret, and we're family. We deserve to know, too—especially now that we have the bakery."

Nana simply chuckled as she reached for a set of oven mitts decorated with cartoon spatulas, mixing bowls, and cookies. They were resting on the counter next to an old juicer that had seen better days. "I'm keeping my eye on you, young man. You'd better not try anything fishy."

Andrew raised a hand in promise, but his slanted grin undermined the gesture. "Perish the thought."

As their grandmother bent over to retrieve the tray from the oven, Andrew met Penny's gaze before looking over toward the gingerbread men cooling on a nearby wire rack.

"I think these have already cooled," Penny announced, pressing the tip of her finger to one of the cookies.

"I'll pack them up for you," Andrew offered, far too eagerly.

"Oh, no, you don't," Betty declared. "Penny?"

"Already on it," she replied.

"Hey, that hurts," Andrew quipped to their grandmother. "Don't you trust me?"

Nana met Andrew's teasing head-on. "Not any farther than I can throw you."

As Andrew and Nana continued their banter, Penny found a container large enough to house the cookies, discreetly slipping a sandwich bag into her jeans pocket as she did so. When she had the opportunity, she diverted a couple of cookies into the bag, alerting Andrew to the capture with a subtle wink.

Catching on, Andrew lifted the lid off a pot that had been patiently awaiting their arrival.

"Mmm, smells good," he said, complimenting their grandmother. "I'll bring this to the table."

"Not without plating it first, you won't," Nana chided, reaching for the soup bowls on a high shelf on tiptoe. "You've all but forgotten your manners in your time away."

"What can I say?" Andrew shrugged. "Eating straight from the pot is the bachelor lifestyle at its finest."

"In that case," Nana returned with an impish grin, "I think it's time we find you a girlfriend."

"Whoa, slow down," Andrew decreed, hands up in partial surrender. "Finding a girlfriend is the absolute *last* thing on my mind."

Nana ignored him, turning her attention to her granddaughter. "What do you think about this, Penny?"

Penny couldn't hold back an amused grin as she watched her brother squirm at the thought. She herself wouldn't be pleased with Nana matchmaking for her. But Andrew's reaction to her suggestion was priceless.

"I'm not opposed to the idea," she played along.

"You know, Anabelle Ryce's granddaughter is just about your age," Nana teased, rubbing her chin as she pretended to muse. "Maybe I'll give her a call."

"Okay, hold on a minute. How about this," Andrew hastily offered. "I'll stop bugging you about your recipe if you back down on this whole matchmaking thing."

Nana's eyes sparkled, a sure sign that she had absolutely no intention of keeping her promise. "It's a deal."

While Nana and Andrew began to set the table for dinner, Penny managed to slip away, tucking the cookies into the inside pocket of her jacket before quietly returning to the kitchen. When Andrew sent a curious glance her way, Penny reassured her brother with a quick nod.

Their plan had worked. She'd managed to nab a few of Nana's famous gingerbread cookies to analyze. All that was left to do now was to solve the mystery.

"This feels a bit like frosting a cake," Penny remarked as she spread mortar over the back of an elongated floor tile.

"Not a cookie?"

Matthew's quick movements as he smoothed mortar over the concrete floor put Penny's attempt to shame. He reached for a tile, then pressed it to the ground after a quick examination and approval of her work.

"Oh, no," Penny replied, pulling another tile from a large box. "We use royal icing for that."

Matthew turned from his position on the floor to shoot a raised eyebrow her way. "English, please?"

"It's a different kind of icing," Penny replied. "It's thinner, and when it sets, it gives a smooth, even finish to the cookie."

"Interesting." Matthew nodded, even though his focus was on the floor.

Penny cocked her head to the side. "You don't sound very interested."

A low chuckle escaped him, sending her heart airborne. "I guess I just prefer eating cookies to decorating them."

"Ain't that the truth." Cassandra breezed into Morgan's unit accompanied by the tinkling of bells, a large box balanced between her hands. "This guy can literally eat his weight in cookies. And he does, especially around the holidays. That's why we nicknamed him Santa Claus."

"Thanks for oversharing, sis," Matthew quipped in response.

Matthew's comment brought a smile to Penny's face. The gesture proved contagious when Matthew stole a glance at her and saw the results of his handiwork.

"My pleasure," came the sassy reply. She set the box down

closer to the entrance. "My wallpaper samples arrived, and I am beyond excited to take a peek. But... I know better than to try and make decisions before my morning coffee. So, what can I get for you both?"

"I'm fine with anything," Matthew replied. "As long as its caffeinated."

Penny felt a twinge of discomfort, remembering her limitations.

"The opposite for me." She tried to sound breezy. "Decaf anything would be great."

"Wow, you two are easy customers," Cassandra laughed. "But I'm not complaining. I'll be back soon."

Then she turned and left.

"What was I saying?" Matthew asked once she was gone.

"We were talking about the difference between royal icing and buttercream."

"Oh, right." A wry smile quirked the corner of his mouth. "How could I have forgotten that?"

"I'll let it slide."

"Thanks," he replied, returning to his work. "So how did you get to know so much about baking, anyway? Didn't you say you worked in marketing before?"

"That would be my mom's influence," Penny answered, feeling a strange mixture of contentedness and grief at the recollection.

"Would she make sky-high cakes for your birthdays or something like that?"

"Something like that," Penny chuckled, resuming her mortar-spreading duties and handing him a tile. "Mom was a wonderful cook, but a terrible baker. Andrew and I decided from a pretty early age that if we wanted to have a decent dessert, we were going to have to make it ourselves."

Matthew laughed. "I guess that's one way to look at it. But who taught you two how to bake, if it wasn't your mom?"

"Nana," Penny answered. "Once we'd moved in with her, a few years after my dad passed."

"How old were you then?"

"Mmm, I think I was six and Andrew was three."

Matthew nodded. "So you've had years of experience."

"You've got that right," Penny replied. "Nana was thrilled to have two pint-sized helpers in the kitchen, and we loved it, too. We made all kinds of treats with her. Cakes, cookies, eclairs…"

"Everything but gingerbread?" he chuckled.

"Right," Penny laughed. "Unfortunately for Andrew and I, that's one recipe she's chosen to keep for herself."

Matthew sat back on his heels to assess his work, then shifted to reach another area of the floor.

"So why didn't you decide to pursue baking as a career earlier?" Matthew's questions continued.

Penny drew in a breath as she thought. That was a good question. Hopefully she could come up with an equally good answer.

"When I left, I… kind of put away anything that would remind me too much of home. I didn't want to think about life here in Cedar Ridge, because remembering hurt too badly."

Matthew nodded in sympathy, glancing up at her from the ground. "I get that."

Did he? Could Matthew really understand how she had felt, how desperately she had needed a fresh start? That was the reason why she had left so suddenly, why she had never looked back or reached out, even though she had missed him terribly in her time away. Could Matthew understand, and more than that, could he forgive? Or was he just being polite?

"So you went in the opposite direction instead," he prompted her.

"Yeah."

Although marketing had still given her an avenue to flex

her creative muscles, an opportunity she would always be grateful for.

"How about Andrew? Is this a new beginning for him, too?"

"Oh, no." Penny shook her head. "Andrew fell in love with baking and stayed the course his entire life. He's classically trained and a much better baker than I am."

Matthew hummed. "It's really interesting how different your two reactions were."

"Well, it won't take you very long to discover that Andrew and I are polar opposites." Penny threw her gaze away. "For him, baking was an outlet and a comfort. For me, it just brought back memories. Good memories," she quickly amended. "But memories that reminded me of what I'd lost."

She paused. He waited.

"You know that saying, 'Don't cry because it's over, smile because it happened?' Andrew took that to heart, but I had a little bit more trouble."

One large hand covered hers, taking her by surprise. When had he sidled closer? She had been so lost in thought, she hadn't noticed.

"Penny, it's okay that you grieved differently than your brother," he consoled her. "There isn't a right or wrong way to grieve. Everybody handles loss differently."

Still avoiding his gaze, Penny turned her attention to his hand resting gently over hers. Talking about the past was hard, but their connection gave her a feeling of comfort and strength.

"Thanks," she mumbled, overcome by a sudden wave of self-consciousness.

"You're welcome," Matthew replied softly. "And, for the record, I'm glad you're back."

Penny sucked in a quick breath.

"Really?"

"It'll be a lot easier to get my cookie fix this way," he joked. "Especially now that you know about my addiction."

Penny laughed, the sound harmonizing with the tinkling of bells that signaled Cassandra's return.

"Don't worry," Penny reassured him. "I already knew all about your cookie addiction."

Matthew's head jerked toward her, his surprise more than evident. "You did?"

"Yeah," she said, biting back a laugh. "Don't you remember buying the youth group out of cookies at our Christmas fundraiser? You'd always start with one, then come back over and over again until we eventually ran out."

"Oh." Surprise suddenly turned to self-consciousness as Matthew's gaze returned to the ground. "Right, I remember now…"

Above them, Cassandra's airy laugh filled in the empty space left behind by his trailing comment.

"Penny, that didn't have anything to do with cookies."

Penny felt the heat of embarrassment steadily creeping up her neck. If she didn't do something soon, her cheeks were about to become redder than Santa's jacket.

"I really like this tile you chose," she offered, hoping to distract the tenacious designer. "It's so cool that it looks like wood."

"Isn't it fantastic?" Cassandra agreed, her matchmaking efforts temporarily forgotten as she walked around to evaluate their progress from every angle. "And this super blond, almost white color… I just love it!"

Cassandra and set down a tray of coffee on the unopened box, then slipped out of her coat and scarf. "All the warmth of a natural wood without needing to worry about water damage. It's the perfect solution for a hair salon."

Cassandra handed Penny a coffee cup.

She hummed an affirmation while surreptitiously sneaking a peek at the side of her cup to make sure the drink was in fact labelled decaf.

"Speaking of work..." Matthew looked up at them both, extending a hand.

"Oh, sorry!" Penny set down her coffee and reached for a tile and trowel. "I'm slacking off."

"Come on, Matt," Cassandra chided her brother. "Progress is going great. You can afford to take a break."

But Matthew ignored his sister, taking the tile Penny offered and pressing it into place. "This schedule is crazy tight as it is," he stated plainly. "And we need to leave time for training now, thanks to you."

Sympathy welled in Penny's heart for the overworked contractor. It had to be exhausting pushing so hard for this Christmas deadline. She wished there was something she could do to help ease his burden. Instead, she realized with a pang of remorse, she was only making it heavier.

Cassandra, on the other hand, far from feeling any guilt about adding to her brother's workload, received his pointed comment as high praise. "I know—I'm a genius. You don't need to say it."

"Good," Matthew jeered. "Because I wasn't planning to."

Penny felt an amused smile tug at her mouth as she listened to their back-and-forth banter. Good old sibling rivalry.

Her smile waned as her thoughts turned to Andrew. How many moments like these had she missed during her time away?

"How is training going, by the way?" Cassandra asked, her voice breaking into Penny's thoughts. "Anything...interesting happen so far?"

Penny fought hard to keep a firm hold on her emotions at her question. She couldn't let Cassandra see how she felt.

For Matthew's sake, of course.

"Nope," she replied, pleased with the cheery yet nonchalant tone she managed to achieve. "Nothing."

The impish gleam that had lit up Cassandra's dark eyes

quickly disappeared at Penny's answer. "Oh," she lamented. "That's too bad." She seemed to lose interest after that, taking a swig of her coffee before reaching for a trowel herself. Penny breathed a sigh of relief.

Safe for now.

But once Cassandra's intense focus was diverted from her target, Penny became acutely aware of another set of eyes boring into her.

Gazing toward Matthew, she found his brow furrowed over stormy eyes, lips pressed tight into a thin line. He didn't look too pleased with her answer, either.

"Is something wrong?" she ventured.

In response, his emerald eyes turned to black. Every hint of vulnerability fled and was replaced with a cool indifference that made her heart feel like it had fallen headlong into a snowdrift.

"Nope," he replied, swiping his trowel across the floor a little more forcefully than before. "Nothing."

To say that Matthew felt out of sorts would be a major understatement. But how else was he supposed to feel, watching Penny set up her equipment in his workshop? Amid the tool-filled, sawdust-scented, and otherwise distinctly masculine space, Penny's radiant beauty shone even more brilliantly than usual. Sporting dark-wash skinny jeans, a pale pink sweater, and a bouncy ponytail, she was the perfect picture of femininity.

He didn't like it one bit.

Mostly because he liked it far too much for his own good.

Matthew hadn't felt this conflicted since...well, ever. Here he was trying hard not to stare, and Penny didn't seem even remotely affected by his presence.

Her words from yesterday still smarted.

Nothing. Is that what he meant to her? What their past

meant? And what about the time they were spending together now? All that... nothing?

Ugh. This was exactly the situation he had been trying to avoid.

"Okay, so I'm going to start by getting some footage of you working," Penny announced brightly, her brow adorably furrowed as she concentrated on clipping her phone into a strange-looking apparatus. "Then we can do a little interview about your artwork and motivation."

Did she just say *interview*? Matthew cast a look down at the worn flannel shirt he had thrown over a white T-shirt and stained work jeans. He was in no shape to be on camera, that's for sure. But even if he was, being the center of attention wasn't what he wanted at all. In fact, it was the opposite.

"What about the artwork itself?" he asked her.

"Oh, of course." Penny reassured him by sending a relaxed smile over her shoulder that set his heart to thumping. "I'll also pan the shop, the grounds, and the artwork, then take some photos for your media library."

"Penny, are you sure all this is necessary?" Matthew ventured tentatively. "All I'm looking for is a functional website."

The rest just seemed like overkill.

"Absolutely!" she said, beaming. "Customers both need and want to connect with a brand before making a purchase, so that means we have to add a personal touch to your site. The more details we can include, the better it'll be, and the better the artwork will sell."

"But this isn't about me." Matthew frowned. "It's about the art."

More specifically, about the man who invented it.

"Well, yes," Penny hedged, clasping her hands together. "But ultimately, your customer's perceived connection with you is what will determine whether they buy your art."

But that was just it—this wasn't his art. It was Mac's. He was just trying to finish what his mentor had started.

"So you're saying that to sell the art, we have to sell *me*?" he clarified. He didn't like the sound of that, for far too many reasons to list.

A thin line appeared between Penny's eyebrows in response to Matthew's challenge. "Well, I wouldn't put it exactly like that."

"How would you put it, then?"

A storm quickly rose in her ocean-blue eyes, deepening them to a hazy sapphire. Clearly, his resistance was proving to be a shock, and an unwelcome one at that. He wasn't trying to be difficult. Unfortunately, he was succeeding.

"Matthew," she began, her soft voice nearly distracting him from the matter at hand. "I understand that this process may seem a bit counterintuitive, but I have helped hundreds of companies cut through the noise and get noticed by consumers, and I can do that for you, too. But in order for this to work, I'm going to need you to trust me."

How did she know exactly what she needed to say to break down his walls?

"It's not that I don't trust you," Matthew said, closing his eyes to buy himself a moment of reprieve from the disappointment he saw scrawled across her face. He hated the thought of disappointing her even more than he hated the thought of being a brand. And that was saying a lot.

"Then what is it?"

Her voice seemed closer now. Opening his eyes, he saw that Penny had stepped forward, her earlier disappointment hastily transformed into concern. For him.

No, he reminded himself. For his *brand*.

"I'm..." He trailed off, unsure of how much he should reveal. "Penny, I'm not interested in being online."

A sympathetic shimmer lent new depths to her already mesmerizing gaze. "That's why you've never had social media."

Matthew nodded. "Right. I'm a private person. I like to keep to myself."

One eyebrow arched along with the corner of her mouth to silently contest that statement. "Could've fooled me."

He exhaled a slow breath. Shoved his hands into his pockets. Then took a step back from the only woman who'd ever managed to draw him out of his shell.

"I know what you're thinking," he said, eyes fixed on the wall beside them. "I was a first rate, high school big shot back in the day, always in the spotlight, so I have no excuse now. Right?"

The resulting silence reluctantly drew his attention back to Penny. Her arms were crossed, and determination swam in those azure eyes. Despite the serious twist in their conversation, he had to fight the urge to smile. The Penny he knew as a teenager hadn't been so self-assured. But he liked the change. It was endearing.

She was endearing.

"I wasn't thinking that at all," Penny revealed, her voice barely a whisper. "I was thinking that's a pretty ironic statement to make, given that you always dominated our conversations."

He laughed at her unexpected revelation.

"I guess that's fair," Matthew admitted, feeling himself relax a bit. "I did tend to get carried away in your company."

"Well, it wasn't entirely your fault," Penny reassured him, a curious look passing over her face. "I wasn't exactly a chatterbox back then."

Was that affection he was seeing? No. Impossible. And yet... He couldn't deny the shimmer of awareness that seemed to be passing between them. Did she feel it, too?

As if suddenly gripped with self-consciousness, Penny

ducked her head and stepped away. But not before he saw the trepidation lurking in her eyes.

"I guess…" She trailed off. "We've both changed a lot since then."

Then, without a second glance his way, she stepped back toward her camera. Her professional demeanor was back, and Matthew felt the disappointment like a physical blow.

"You were the exception, you know."

Startled, Penny whirled around. "What?"

Why had he told her that? Because, he realized belatedly, he wanted to keep the old Penny around a little while longer.

"You were the exception," he repeated, more decisively this time. "I didn't open up to everyone. Just you."

Penny's expression didn't change, but her shoulders seemed to soften as she nodded slowly. Eyes downcast, she didn't say a word. She simply resumed her work behind the camera.

"I'll start with the artwork today," she announced, a subtle waver undermining her attempt at an even monotone. "That'll give you some time to think things over. Then we can shoot the interview whenever you're ready."

A hollow feeling settled in his heart, in the same place where that tiny flicker of hope he'd been holding on to had once briefly resided.

What had he been thinking?

Honestly, he hadn't been thinking. He'd been feeling something familiar and comforting. But obviously, that was just his imagination gone rogue. Whatever feelings Penny may have had for him were now clearly ancient history.

Matthew supposed he should be grateful for the reality check. Unfortunately, the only gratitude he could muster was for the brief glimpse he'd been given into their past. Because as much as Matthew tried to convince himself otherwise, the simple fact was, he missed Penny. The Penny he used to know. The Penny he had fallen in love with.

Not that he had ever told her that.

Matthew balled his hands into fists to keep from running them across his face. How much longer until the contest? Just about two more weeks.

At this point, that was feeling like two weeks too many.

Penny pressed two open palms against tired eyes later that evening.

Too much screen time. And not nearly enough to show for it.

She had spent the last few hours meticulously editing the pictures she had taken at Matthew's workshop. But all the adjustments in the world weren't going to make up for the fact that they were only pictures of wood and tools.

Penny closed her laptop and sat back in her seat, as she ran through the events of the day. It wasn't impossible to market Matthew's artwork on its own. The ingenious shapes, colors, and compositions spoke for themselves. But, she reluctantly realized, her entire marketing strategy revolved around the brooding artist.

Her game plan didn't mean anything other than that personal stories tend to be very well received by consumers. The fact that she wanted to fill in the gaps in Matthew's history to satisfy her own curiosity had absolutely nothing to do with it.

Penny scoffed. Not even she believed her own futile protest.

Okay, so she was curious about Matthew's story. That was a perfectly reasonable response toward someone she hadn't seen in a long time. Right?

You were the exception.

To say that that innocent comment of his had thrown her off balance would be like calling a blizzard a snowfall. But, she reminded herself sternly, that was a long time ago, and they weren't kids anymore. Matthew had simply been reminiscing, nothing more.

So why did she secretly want it to be something more?

No, she asserted, that couldn't happen. She was unavailable, to everyone. Her health would make sure of that.

Penny tightly gripped the arms of her chair. It just wasn't fair that she had no say in the matter. Why had that decision been taken away from her? Why had she been dealt this terrible hand? What in the world was God doing?

Guilt nearly made her wince. To get away from it, she stood and started to pace.

Maybe if she hadn't stopped going to church or reading her Bible, she'd know the answer to that question. Instead, her meagre attempts at prayer were feeling very much like too little, too late.

Voices from the first floor broke into her spinning thoughts.

"Thank you so much for coming," Nana said to someone. "I can't wait to give you the grand tour."

"Thank you, Betty," another female voice replied. "I have to say, I was very surprised when you called me, but I'm so glad you chose to trust me with this sale."

Penny froze, then quickly scurried to the landing once the shock wore off.

"Oh, Caroline," Nana continued. "Who else would I call? You're not only my friend, you're the perfect person for the job."

Caroline. As in, Caroline Thompson, Morgan's grandmother and Nana's bridge partner. Who also happened to be the top-selling Realtor in the county.

What was going on?

"You know, it was so funny the way this worked out," Caroline began. "Right before you called me, I had just gotten off the phone with a sweet couple from Ann Arbor looking to retire in the country. I think this house would be a perfect fit for them."

Penny gasped. Caroline already had a potential buyer? How was she supposed to compete with that?

"Oh, how wonderful!" Nana exclaimed, with a joyful clap thrown in for good measure. "When are they planning to move?"

"The sooner the better, in their words."

Penny closed her eyes and buried her face in her hands. This was very, very bad.

What was she going to do?

Chapter Five

"Time."

Matthew was more than a little reluctant to end Penny's latest baking practice run, but even after giving her an extra five minutes, her gingerbread Christmas tree was still nowhere near completed.

Penny stopped and blew out a frustrated huff, sending a few errant wisps of hair floating away momentarily before they landed messily across her face. "Well, that was brutal."

Brutal might not be exactly the word Matthew would use to describe this evening's lackluster performance, but after watching her confidence growing steadily over the last while, he had to admit, they were beginning to move backward.

"Is everything okay?" he ventured. "You seem out of sorts today."

"Yeah, I noticed," she murmured, plunking one hand on her hip and using the other to brush away those stray locks. Her expression wavered between disgust and disappointment as she surveyed the lopsided cookie display. "This is ridiculous. I should be much further along than this by now."

Matthew recognized dejection when he heard it. He had to nip that in the bud, and fast. An impromptu pity party would only set them back.

"Don't say that," he implored her, calling on his inner

coach. "There aren't any *shoulds* here. It's about progress, not perfection."

The unimpressed glance she leveled him with told him that she wasn't convinced just yet.

"Fine," she said, a petulant edge undermining her otherwise agreeable words. "But surely you can see that I'm not progressing."

"Hey." Matthew stepped closer, then lightly grasped her arms. He had to get her out of this funk. "Stop that. One bad day does not mean it's game over."

Despite his proximity, Penny stayed laser-focused on the tragic Christmas tree, but the steadily deepening color of her cheeks gave her away.

He tucked a finger under her chin and gently turned her head toward him. "Do you believe me?"

The movement caused an unexpected shift in her demeanor. Frustration fell away to reveal wide, watery eyes and a trembling mouth.

"I want to."

Her shaky voice seemed disproportionately fragile, given the circumstances. This couldn't just be about cookies. Clearly, something else was bothering her.

"What's going on?" he asked.

She hesitated, biting her lower lip to keep from speaking. Or maybe crying?

"You can trust me, Penny," he added, after what felt like a very long minute.

"I know." Her response was quiet, but immediate. Certain. It caused a pleasant warmth to settle in Matthew's chest, knowing that she still felt safe around him.

"Nana…" she continued, visibly struggling to stay composed. "She's…"

Tears began to spill over onto her cheeks. Unthinkingly, he pulled her into his arms and held her close as her body shook with emotion. "It's okay," he murmured, running a reassuring hand along her back. "I've got you."

They stood there for some time, the only sounds Penny's muffled sobs accompanied by the rapid pounding in his chest. As he held her, all his defenses fell away as the protective instincts he'd been fighting to hold at bay came rushing back, full force.

Matthew's heart ached as he held her. He wanted nothing more than to ease her burden, to take away whatever it was that was bothering her.

To come to her rescue again.

Those were dangerous thoughts and he knew it, but Matthew couldn't deny the truth. His heart wouldn't allow it. He cared for Penny. He probably always would. And whether or not she ever felt the same, Matthew resolved then and there to get to the bottom of things, to discover her problem and fix it.

Not that he had any right to do so. Not that he was anything other than a coach to her. But how could he not want to intervene, when Penny was so distraught? If nothing else, it was the right thing to do. At least, that's what he told himself.

"I'm sorry," she eventually mumbled, pulling away to wipe the backs of her hands across her tearstained face.

Matthew's heart swelled at the sight. In spite of her messy bun, the flecks of mascara that dotted her cheeks, and her red-rimmed eyes, Penny was more beautiful now than he'd ever seen her. She was vulnerable. She was *real*.

"Don't apologize," he breathed, gently helping her wipe tears from her face.

Her breath caught at his touch, and her whole body froze for a moment before relaxing on a shaky exhale. Undaunted, Matthew turned his attention to the stray wisps of her hair. He gently tucked them behind her ear while allowing his eyes to roam freely across her delicate features.

They were close. Close enough that he could see the faint

smattering of freckles that lightly dusted her cheeks. Close enough to breathe in her comforting vanilla scent.

His eyes lingered on her mouth for just a moment before he dragged them back up to hers. If Penny had noticed, she didn't seem bothered by it. On the contrary, her gaze was soft and serene, glowing with an unspoken affection that sent his heart soaring.

But Matthew knew that getting too close too fast wouldn't be good for either of them. He'd made that mistake once before, believing that Penny had felt something for him only to find out the hard way that he was wrong. That wasn't something he wanted to repeat anytime soon.

He forced himself to lean back. Then he cleared his throat.

"Why don't we sit down and talk," he suggested.

Penny blinked, then slowly nodded, as if taking her time waking up from a dream. "Okay."

He led her to the second worktable and pulled out the two stools tucked away underneath.

"What I had been trying to say," Penny began, shifting in her seat, "is that Nana is…selling her house." She took a deep breath, eyes closed, before continuing. "I want to buy it, but I don't have enough money."

Understanding finally clicked. "Which is why you're so invested in this contest."

"Yes," she admitted, clasping her hands together in her lap. "I know it sounds silly, but I'm just not ready to let it go. Even when I was away, I always found it comforting to know that Mom…" She stopped. "That my mother's memories still lived on there, in the house."

"It's not silly," Matthew countered, leaning forward slightly to rest his elbows on his knees. "It makes a lot of sense, actually."

That was exactly the same way he felt about Mac. Spaces in his home or items in the workshop could trigger memories at the strangest times. They were like little gifts scattered throughout the day. The odd mix of wistful nostalgia and joyful recollection they elicited had sustained him during the hard times.

That realization stopped him short. When had Matthew started thinking of the hard times as something in his past?

"I'm sorry about the house," he offered, choosing to tuck that question away for future recollection. "That must have been a rough start to your homecoming."

"Yeah, you could say that," she sighed, keeping her gaze fixed on the concrete floor. "It seems like I left a lot of unfinished business around here."

Matthew's heart foolishly leaped to attention. "Like what?"

Her eyes rose to meet his and held them captive, but try as he might, Matthew couldn't decipher the source of the sadness he saw in them. When she spoke, he had to strain to hear her words. "When I left, I thought I was getting away from the things that scared me. Turns out, those things have a funny way of following you around until you face them."

Matthew felt his body relax on a breath he hadn't realized he'd been holding.

She hadn't been talking about him.

He tried to tell himself that it didn't matter. But if that was the case, why did he feel so disappointed?

"I never made peace with my mom's death," Penny confessed, dropping her gaze to her intertwined fingers. "It sounds odd to say out loud, but somehow, in my mind, leaving meant that she was still here, and I was just away on vacation."

"So that's the real reason why you never came home?"

"Yeah." She released a breathy laugh. "Ridiculous, isn't it?"

"Maybe a little," he acknowledged. "But I get it."

She turned toward him then, her curiosity on full display. "You do?"

He held her gaze for a while before answering, not sure of

what he should say, of why he had even opened that door in the first place.

Matthew didn't talk about Mac. Ever. Sure, people had asked, but he'd become skilled at dodging their questions, until eventually, the questions stopped coming.

Until now.

But instead of feeling the need to abruptly change the topic or rush off, today Matthew found himself wanting to open up.

It wasn't lost on him that the reason for this sudden change had everything to do with the beautiful woman seated across from him. He wasn't sure if that was a good or a bad thing. He also wasn't sure it was wise of him to be spending so much time with her, but that was exactly what he was doing.

Only one thing he knew for absolute certain: something inside of him was pushing Matthew toward hope. Toward Penny. Toward healing, forgiveness, and maybe even a second chance.

And he was scared to death of it.

"Yeah," Matthew finally confirmed. "I do."

Unaware of his inner turmoil, Penny simply nodded her head slowly, as if trying to figure him out. He could tell she was intrigued, but he also knew she wouldn't push. Penny had never been one to insist, only to support. It was one of the countless reasons why he'd fallen for her.

When he didn't offer more, Penny picked up her earlier thread. "Now that I'm back, it just feels like I'm not going to have enough time to find her again."

"That isn't how it works," Matthew interjected. "Memories have a way of sneaking up on you when you least expect them."

Penny didn't respond, but her eyes narrowed ever so slightly as she considered him. Matthew had a feeling he was about to get hit with a question he wasn't yet ready to answer. Now would be a good time for him to revert to his old habits and deflect.

"So what made you come home after all?" he asked. "Why was now the right time?"

Her face fell, along with her shoulders, but she quickly pulled herself together. Not fast enough, however, to hide the trepidation that had flashed through her eyes. The unusual reaction shook him to the core.

Matthew hadn't been expecting that. He thought she might reference the Returning Residents program, Andrew's invitation, or some other hometown appeal. But that look made him suspect that she might not have come back *for* something, after all. Maybe she was running *from* something.

Again.

But what could be so bad as to drive her back to a place that she had once deserted in the name of self-preservation?

A cold dread began to creep up the length of his spine, sending any caution he had managed to muster flying straight out the window.

It seemed like his earlier suspicion was right. Something was wrong. Very wrong.

And he was going to figure out what it was.

"There you are," Penny whispered as she spied the large leather photo album buried behind stacks of books in the bottom cabinet of the credenza. Pushing the volumes aside, she kneeled down, reached in, and proceeded to wiggle the hefty tome this way and that, rejoicing once she had it in her arms.

Anticipation built as she ran a reverent hand over the embossed front cover. She hadn't seen these photos in years. And while Matthew's opinion about memories was certainly valid, Penny couldn't help herself from wanting to take the opposite approach. Instead of waiting for memories to find her, she was seeking them out herself.

To say that she'd been surprised by his insight into how she was feeling would be an understatement. He spoke as if he understood her loss, but as far as she knew, both of his parents were still alive. Who else might he be mourning?

A spouse?

Her heart gave a painful squeeze at the thought of Matthew with another woman. Nope, that didn't sit well with her. Matthew hurting...that was a thought she liked even less.

Penny shook her head to disentangle it from her musings. Matthew's private life was none of her concern. She was his business partner, nothing more. No longer his friend and confidante. And certainly not his girlfriend.

Too bad the other night had felt anything but platonic. When life overwhelmed her, Matthew protected and cared for her better than any boyfriend she'd ever had. For the briefest of moments, she'd even thought that he wanted...

No. She wouldn't allow herself to go there. It wasn't possible.

It *couldn't* be possible. Not with her heart still hanging in the balance.

Making her way to the sitting room by the front window, Penny resolved to focus on the here and now. To take in all the sights and sounds of her childhood home while finally making peace with her past. Plunking onto the well-worn love seat, she took a deep breath and drank in the moment.

Nearby, the fragrant scent of the still-bare Christmas tree tickled her nose. Combined with the sugar-cookie-scented candle burning nearby, it created a unique fragrance that perfectly embodied the holidays.

From its place beside the sofa, an antique lamp offered light low enough that she could see a field of pristine white snow through the window. Superimposed onto the scene were a couple of kids ambitiously trying to construct a veritable snow fortress. Just then, a memory surfaced. She wondered whether Andrew might be coerced into reliving their snow-man-building days, then she chuckled when she imagined the updated attempt in her mind.

She was almost ready. There was just one thing missing. Rising, Penny opened the old record player that sat by the window. She chose an LP, dropped the needle, then stepped back as instrumental Christmas music began to play.

Now, everything was perfect.

Well, everything except her red-reindeer pajama pants and fuzzy pink slippers. They would do for tonight, but she would be sure to trade them in for some more photogenic attire before the tree-decorating party Nana would be hosting on Saturday. Besides, she thought as she curled up on the sofa, it wasn't like anyone would see them under the chunky knit blanket she draped over her legs.

Time passed unnoticed as the photo album took her on a journey through the years, stopping at school plays, road trips, summer picnics, and family holidays. Some memories were so silly they made her laugh out loud. Others drew wistful tears to her eyes as she reminisced.

As Penny turned the page, a photo slipped out and landed on her lap. The image stopped her heart.

"Oh, wow."

A candid photograph of her mother on her wedding day. Penny held her breath as she reached for the picture and held it with trembling fingers. Standing before her vanity, the beaming bride was looking over her shoulder and laughing at the photographer. A lump formed in Penny's throat at the sight.

"Oh, Mom, you are so beautiful."

As she studied the photo, more details began to surface. The simple lace gown that flared gently around her feet. The letter in her mother's hands, presumably from her groom-to-be. The faint reflection in the mirror of her late grandfather standing beside an already watery-eyed Nana. Then the details began to blur, obscured by a flood of tears.

"I wish you could be here for my wedding," Penny whispered.

If she ever got to have one, that is.

Penny sighed as she swiped at her eyes. The constant stream of what-ifs were slowly but surely wearing her down, acting as a persistent foil for the hope that she so ardently wanted to nurture. She wanted to have faith, to believe that things would be all right, but fear and doubt were proving to be a formidable duo, causing Penny to feel as though she was caught in a never-ending game of tug-of-war.

"How did you handle this with such grace?" she asked, addressing her mother in the picture. "How were you so at peace with your condition?"

Penny had just turned fifteen when Elizabeth Shay was diagnosed with hypertrophic cardiomyopathy. And while there had certainly been an adjustment period for the family, her mother had refused to wallow in self-pity for very long. The initial shock and grief had quickly given way to a resolute bravado. Yes, Elizabeth Shay had been knocked over by the news, but she hadn't stayed down for long. She insisted on enjoying life to the fullest, refusing to let her illness define her.

As she reflected on her mother's example, hope gained the upper hand.

Could she somehow find the strength to do the same?

A knock on the window jolted her out of her reverie, sending her pulse skyrocketing. The sight of Matthew waving on the other side of the window, a tray of take-out coffee containers in hand, did nothing to bring it back down to earth.

After setting aside the album and blanket, Penny got up to open the front door for him.

"Hey." His eyebrows rose and his smile widened as he noticed her pajama pants and slippers. He let out a low whistle. "Wow. You look—"

"Not a word," she ordered, holding up a finger to stop him. "I don't want to hear it."

"Really?" He leaned against the doorframe, a playful smile creating a cute little dimple in his cheek. "Are you sure?"

Penny wasn't sure of anything as far as Matthew was concerned.

"Positive."

"All right, fine," he practically drawled, his lowered voice waking the butterflies that had taken up residence in her stomach. "In that case, I won't tell you how cute you look."

Penny's jaw dropped at the unexpected comment. Matthew grinned, clearly pleased with her reaction.

"So are you going to invite me in?" he asked, holding up the coffee cups. "I come bearing gifts."

"Oh, right." Penny's mind did a quick jump start as she stepped aside. "Come on in."

"Thanks." He wiped his feet on the welcome mat before stepping inside. "I hope you're still a fan of white hot chocolate."

Penny's breath caught in her throat, but she pushed herself past it as she closed the door. "You remembered."

"Right down to the crushed candy canes on top."

Penny gratefully accepted the festive drink, feeling her already feeble defenses beginning to fall away in the face of such touching thoughtfulness.

"I couldn't resist getting this for your grandmother," Matthew continued. "Gingerbread-spiced hot chocolate. Pretty appropriate, don't you think?"

A quick laugh escaped Penny's lips. "Oh, you don't know the half of it."

An endearing spark brought his emerald eyes to life. "Want to tell me the rest?"

Matthew's expression was open, his smile warmer than the cup held between her hands. Penny found herself smiling in return. She liked this relaxed side of him. Probably a little too much for her own good.

Looking back over her shoulder to make sure Nana wouldn't

overhear, Penny leaned forward and whispered, "Andrew and I are working on solving the mystery of Nana's secret gingerbread recipe."

Matthew's eyebrow rose in intrigue. "And? How's it been going? Any leads so far?"

"Not yet," she answered. "But we still have time. Andrew thinks it would help us win the contest."

"Maybe," Matthew agreed. "Personally, I think your newfound construction skills are what's going to give you an edge."

"I'm getting that good, huh?" Penny joked.

"Oh yeah," Matthew grinned.

"Must be all that work my coach has been putting in with me."

"Definitely," he deadpanned. "I hear he's the best in the business."

Penny laughed, then nodded to the tray of coffee.

"What about the third cup?" she asked.

"That's mine." Matthew cast a quick glance at the drink in question, then sheepishly replied, "I thought I might grab one, too, just in case."

Just in case...what? Why was Matthew paying her this visit? Was it possible that she hadn't imagined things? That he still had feelings for her?

Penny's traitorous heart immediately kicked into overdrive at the thought of her long-abandoned dream come true. But the intense throbbing in her chest was also a stark reminder of why a relationship with Matthew was out of the question. If it kept beating at this rate, she'd have to sit down soon, before the dizziness crept in.

Before he noticed that something was wrong.

"Are you planning to stay a while?" she asked, keeping her voice as even as possible.

"If it's not too much of an intrusion." Matthew shrugged, suddenly adorably shy. "But if you're in the middle of something, then—"

"No, no," she hastily protested, surprised at her resistance to the thought of him leaving so soon. "It's nothing, I was just looking through some old photos. Would you like to join me?"

"I'd love to."

An easy smile crinkled the corners of his eyes—eyes that glowed with an unspoken emotion that called to Penny and drew her in, despite herself. Biting her tongue, she managed to restrain a dreamy sigh from escaping her lips. Honestly, how was she supposed to resist when he was looking at her with such...

What exactly *was* that look lingering in his eyes?

"It sounds like we have a visitor." Nana's cheerful tone entered the room before she did. When she caught sight of their guest, she lit up like a jumble of string lights. "Matthew! What a pleasant surprise."

"Hi, Mrs. Nesbitt." Matthew greeted her grandmother with a one-armed hug before handing her her treat.

"Oh, how thoughtful!" Nana aimed a megawatt smile in Matthew's direction.

"It was nothing," Matthew shrugged. "I saw this drink on David's holiday menu and thought of you."

"Well, isn't that just the sweetest thing." Nana stopped fiddling with the silver bun perched precariously atop her head to take the cup he offered her. When she did, Nana aimed a mischievous glance at her granddaughter.

"Hold on to this one, Penny," she advised sagely, a mischievous twinkle passing through her pale blue gaze. "He's a keeper."

If there was any part of her that hadn't yet turned bright red from embarrassment, that comment definitely would have sealed the deal. Penny was absolutely mortified.

"Nana," she insisted, giving her grandmother a stern look behind Matthew's back.

Nana simply chuckled at the warning. "That sounds like

my cue to leave," she announced. "If you two need me, I'll be in the kitchen."

Matthew waited until she was out of earshot, then innocently remarked, "I like your grandmother."

Penny scoffed. "Gee, I wonder why."

If there was a Matthew Banks fan club, Nana would be its president.

Matthew laughed. "Cut her some slack. She's been so lonely around here without you and Andrew to dote on that she's kind of adopted me. I'm sure she's thrilled to have you back."

Penny instantly sobered at the revelation. "Wait. Nana was lonely?"

Matthew's lips flattened into a grim line. "Whoops. Maybe I shouldn't have told you that."

"No, I'm glad that you did," Penny replied. "I'm just surprised, that's all."

Nana had never been one to complain, but it pained her to think that she could have so easily fooled Penny during their phone calls.

Actually, if Penny was being honest, she had to admit she'd been more than a little distracted during her time away. If Nana had dropped any hints as to how she was feeling, Penny probably wouldn't have noticed. She had been far too busy filling her life with endless work projects and diversions to think too much about why she was working so hard. Or to realize that she was needed somewhere else.

"Hey, it's not all bad," Matthew continued. "It's not like she was living in complete isolation. Town is just a few minutes away, and she has lots of friends there."

A sinking feeling settled in the pit of her stomach as a realization finally dawned on Penny.

This was why Nana was selling and moving closer to town.

"I feel awful," Penny confessed. "I should have come home sooner."

"Don't say that," Matthew reassured her. "You obviously didn't know."

No, she hadn't. She had been willfully oblivious, and completely focused on herself.

"But I should have," she insisted. "I mean, what kind of person—"

She stopped herself but the question resounded in her mind.

What kind of person abandons her own family?

"The kind of person that's in pain," Matthew said, providing the answer. "You're not a bad person, Penny. You were just hurting."

She met his gaze and found compassion there, on full display.

"I promise—Betty's fine. She spends time with her friends and volunteers at the church. And once I got back, I checked in on her almost every day."

Penny's ears perked up at that.

Wait…wasn't Matthew a returning resident too?

"When was that?"

He gave her a sheepish smile once he realized he'd slipped.

Caught red-handed.

"Ah, just about seven years ago, now."

Seven years? But that would mean…

"Come on." Matthew gestured to the photo album lying on the couch before claiming a seat on the sofa. "How about you show me what you've found?"

Penny considered pressing the issue, but decided against it. If Matthew wasn't ready to share, she wouldn't insist. No matter how badly she wanted to know the details.

He lifted the album off her side of the couch and allowed her to get settled. As she did, Penny noticed the scent of fresh-cut wood and laundry detergent. How different from the designer colognes all her exes had worn to go along with their expensive custom suits.

She nearly rolled her eyes at the recollection. The men

Penny had chosen to spend her time with were smooth and slick, but those relationships had only been skin-deep. What a contrast to Matthew's relaxed jeans-and-flannel vibe. With him, there was no pretense or facade. He was just a good man with an equally good heart. Seated beside him, Penny felt completely comfortable. Completely herself.

After setting her drink down on the side table, Penny took the blanket and proceeded to fuss with it. As if worrying the covering would somehow dislodge the contented feeling that had settled over her heart. As much as she wanted to, she knew she couldn't dwell on it, not even for a minute. Linking Matthew with a feeling of home was dangerous. She had to be more careful.

"Here."

Penny's heart skipped a beat as Matthew took one side of the blanket from her hands, brushing her fingers lightly as he did. Then it resumed its breakneck speed as he spread the covering over them both.

It felt a lot like something a couple would do.

The sofa suddenly seemed a whole lot smaller, and the room a whole lot cozier, now that she was sharing it with Matthew.

Penny gave herself a firm mental shake. Talk about dangerous thoughts!

Matthew lowered the photo album onto the blanket between them, then leaned in closer.

Their eyes met and held. If he was waiting for a response, he was about to be sorely disappointed. Penny could barely breathe, much less string together a coherent sentence.

How had she gotten herself into this mess? And more importantly, why was she in no hurry to get out of it?

"Hey, look at this." Matthew reached for the photo of Elizabeth, which Penny had yet to return to the album. He studied it with a fondness that turned her racing heart to mush. "That's a great shot."

"Yeah." Her sudden timidity made the word sound smaller than intended. "It's my new favorite."

"I can see why. It perfectly embodies your mom."

"I think so, too," Penny agreed. "She dealt with so much, but she was always so carefree. I've been wondering a lot lately about how that could have been possible."

"It's a fair question," Matthew said. "Especially given how much you've got on your plate right now."

"That goes for both of us," Penny reminded him. "My schedule looks downright breezy compared to yours."

Matthew chuckled. "Yes, well, I seem to have a bad habit of taking on too much."

She could definitely relate.

"Why is that?" she asked.

Matthew shifted in his seat. "I guess in some way it's easier to just keep hopping from one thing to the next. If I stay busy, I don't have to think too much."

Penny hummed an assent. She wondered what exactly he was trying to avoid thinking about.

"Or maybe I'm just trying to prove myself," he admitted, his voice now muted.

"To who?" Penny asked, although she suspected she already knew the answer.

"The answer I want to give is myself," Matthew replied. "But I suspect that the real answer is my father."

Penny nodded. She remembered Matthew's father as having sky-high hopes for his son. She wondered about their relationship now.

But before she could give voice to her unspoken questions, Matthew shifted, his smile growing wider as he held the picture up beside her. Emerald eyes jumped from past to present as he drew a comparison between the two.

"You look like your mom," he finally declared.

"You think so?"

"Oh, yeah," he returned, turning the picture back to face her. "I mean, the eyes are all Andrew, but your mouth and nose are almost identical."

Penny considered the photo anew. "I guess I never noticed that. I was always told I look more like my dad, not that I remember him all that well. From the pictures I've seen, he had darker eyes, too, but they were more gray than blue."

"Maybe it's your personality, then," Matthew continued. "You're just as kind and caring as your mom was."

Penny's heart softened, and she felt a smile spread across her face. "Thanks. That means a lot."

"No problem," he replied. "It's true."

Penny drew in a quick breath at his comment. It couldn't be just her imagination playing tricks on her. Matthew had to be feeling this connection, this draw, between them, too.

"Matthew," she whispered, afraid to break whatever spell they both were under.

"Yeah?" His voice was rich and low.

"Why did you come by tonight?"

He blinked, a melancholy note entering his gaze. "I just wanted to make sure you were okay. You know, after yesterday."

Penny nodded, not trusting herself to speak.

"Are you feeling better?" he asked.

Besides her weakened heart and troubled soul? Yes, she realized with remarkable clarity, she was. Better than she had been in a very long time.

"I am now."

Relief flooded his expression and warmed her tremulous heart.

"Good."

Chapter Six

Matthew was skating on thin ice, and he knew it. But he wasn't about to turn back now. He couldn't. Not when he was cuddled up with Penny like this. Not when they were sharing memories that brought him back to a time before heartbreak and grief. And certainly not when she seemed just as affected by his nearness as he was by hers.

He didn't know what had changed between them. Maybe something had shifted after that moment in the bakery, but Matthew hadn't seen Penny this vulnerable since, well…since high school. For the first time since she returned, he felt like he was talking with the real Penny. Not the polished professional who kept the world at arm's length, but the genuine woman whose every fretful little breath made his heart melt even more.

It wouldn't take anything for him to drape an arm along the back of the couch. Or better yet, around her shoulders. His hands ached to draw her even closer than she was, to close the minuscule gap between them and pick up where they left off all those years ago.

Would she feel the same way if he did? Or would that distant and reserved side of her come rushing back full force? Her shallow breath and airy tone certainly made him hope for the former. But the gnawing doubt in the back of his mind refused to relent, even now.

She left you once before.

Yes, he admitted, but things were different now. They weren't kids anymore, and Penny had come home to stay. He didn't have anything to fear this time.

Right?

As much as he wanted to believe that, Matthew couldn't ignore the fear he had seen in her eyes last night. And until he got to the bottom of that, he couldn't cross any lines, no matter how sorely he was tempted.

"Wow," he commented, pointing to a shot of Penny and Andrew, laughing up a storm on their front porch. Behind them, a banner read, 'First Day of School.' "I don't think I've ever been that excited to go to school."

Penny laughed, a breathy sound that tantalized his senses.

"I don't remember exactly what he did," she mused. "But I know that Andrew was fooling around, trying to make Mom laugh."

"Looks like he succeeded."

"I don't know…" Penny hesitated, her eyes soft as they scanned the picture. "Mom was one tough cookie, pun very much intended. She could hold a poker face better than anyone I know."

Her features softened as fond recollections illuminated her expression from the inside out.

"It even became a kind of contest between them," she explained. "The more Andrew tried to make her laugh, the more resolute Mom became. But every once in a while, he managed to get the best of her."

Matthew chuckled. "I never would have guessed."

Though he had only met Elizabeth Shay a couple of times before she passed away, to Matthew she seemed to be just as open and sincere as her daughter. Unbeknownst to him, it sounded like she had a mischievous side, too.

Penny began to turn the page, then abruptly slammed it back down.

"Oh, no," she exclaimed. "Not that."

"What?" Matthew had been too busy admiring the way the dim light fell across her features to notice the offending photograph. "Let me see."

"No way."

She pulled the album toward her, but he held on tight. "Come on, I'm sure it's not that bad."

"Oh, believe me," she insisted, the rosy pink of her cheeks testifying to her find. "It is."

Matthew slipped a finger between the pages, but she quickly nipped that attempt in the bud.

"Stop!" she laughed, leaning over to cover his hand with hers. But when she realized just how close that action had brought them, all the humor fled from her face, chased away on a swift gasp. She moved to lean back, but Matthew caught her hand and held her there.

"Don't..."

He wanted to say more, but the words died in his throat.

Don't go. Don't withdraw again. Not tonight. Not ever.

The force of his reaction hit Matthew hard. How was it possible that he still felt so strongly for her? Being with Penny now, it was as if all those years apart had never even happened. All the emotions he thought he'd left behind had only been hiding, tucked away in some abject corner of his heart, just waiting for the right moment to resurface. And now that they had, could he really find it in him to ignore them?

Penny swallowed hard, then nodded. "Okay."

She tugged her hand against his and reluctantly, he let her go. When he did, she abandoned the photo album and inched away, back to her side of the couch. He felt the loss like a physical blow.

"Go ahead," she said, and nodded.

He blinked, then refocused. She was talking about the picture. But it didn't mean a thing without her.

"Come back," he said quietly, offering her the album. "I'll behave. I promise."

The caution in her eyes quickly morphed into compassion.

"No," she protested, though she remained firmly in place. "I overreacted. I'm sorry."

"Only because I was being difficult," Matthew countered.

"Yeah, well..." An impish grin spread across her face. "I guess I should be used to that by now."

A quick laugh escaped him. "Ouch."

Penny's lilting chuckle reassured him that the tense moment was behind them.

"Okay, don't drag it out now." She pointed to the photo album. "Quick and painless, like a Band-Aid."

Matthew smirked at the comparison. "I can't imagine what could possibly—" But as he turned the page and came face-to-face with the source of her embarrassment, his words stopped short. "Oh, I can't believe you still have this."

Looking back up at him was...him. Smiling wide as he looked up into the camera, his arm around a far less confident—and far more festively clad—Penny. The scene was the church's annual Breakfast with Santa, the year that Penny had been "voluntold" to play the part of Santa's elf.

"I know," she groaned, burying her face in her hands while still leaving a tiny space between her fingers to peek through. "That costume was so terrible. Candy-cane tights and all."

"Could have been worse," he said, goading her. "You could have had jingle bell shoes to go with those tights."

Penny closed her eyes and waved a hand against the imagery. "No, never!"

Matthew shook his head at her antics, his gaze returning to the image of her seventeen-year-old self. Shy and sweet,

Penny was a natural beauty, and that was something that no costume, no matter how garish, could ever take away.

"Come on, it wasn't all *that* bad," he insisted.

On the contrary, it was absolutely adorable. Which was exactly why Matthew had made it his mission to capture the moment by taking a photo with her. At the time, she hadn't been too enthusiastic about immortalizing the experience in film, but the fact that she still had this picture had to mean something, didn't it?

Penny just smiled and shook her head. "You're too much."

Her words hit a soft spot in his heart.

"Better too much than not enough, I guess."

Her face fell at his observation. "Who told you that you're not enough?"

The indignation shining in her beautiful blue eyes proved enough to revive his temporarily drooping spirit. Matthew liked the thought of her going to bat for him. It was just as adorable as her elf costume.

"Ah, it's nothing," he said, deflecting, and opting to wave off his earlier comment. "Forget that I said anything."

"I don't believe that for a minute," Penny announced, straightening in her seat. "And you shouldn't take those kinds of comments to heart. You're more than enough, Matthew Banks. Don't you dare let anyone tell you otherwise."

Matthew raised an eyebrow, along with the sides of his lips, at the unexpectedly passionate sermon. "Wow, where did that come from?"

Penny shifted, her momentary bravado seemingly shaken by the challenge. But soon enough, she set her jaw and found her footing.

"My heart," she replied, the slight crack in her voice undermining her attempt at self-assurance. "That's where."

It was a good thing Penny had retreated to the far end of the sofa. Otherwise, Matthew might have been tempted to reach for her hand. Or cup her cheek. Or do something even more recklessly stupid.

"You have a good heart," he finally said. It was one of the things he loved most about her.

Penny made a derisive sound and flicked her gaze to the floor. Arms crossed, she said, "That's not something I hear too often anymore."

Matthew's anger was swiftly kindled. What kind of moron would ever want to make Penny feel less than? It wasn't right, and she needed to know that.

"Well, you should."

Their eyes met and held, revealing a sadness he hadn't noticed in her before. Matthew sent up a silent prayer for guidance.

Lord, please let my next words be a reflection of Your love.

"Penny, you've got the purest, most radiantly beautiful heart of everyone I've ever met, and if someone can't see that, it's their loss."

Surprise registered at his words. Wide eyes and a slack jaw told him she had not seen that coming. Nor did she seem to know what to make of his compliment.

Great.

Had he messed things up again? Said too much? Or revealed too much of his own heart in that emphatic statement?

"Thank you."

Penny's quiet response called him out of his thought spiral.

"You're welcome." Then, after a moment, he added, "It's true."

The edges of her mouth quirked up, but before she could say anything more, a loud click broke into the moment, drawing their attention to the doorway.

"Oh, that's a good one." Betty Nesbitt looked down at her phone, clearly pleased with the image on her screen.

"Nana? What are you doing?"

"Taking another photo for the album, of course," Betty said triumphantly. "You two just looked so sweet, making eyes at each other. I couldn't resist!"

Matthew cast a glance at Penny to find her looking more uncomfortable by the minute. "Nana," she complained. "It's not what it looks like... I mean, we're not..."

She shot him a pleading look. Or was it uncertainty? He wasn't sure, but since he couldn't decipher her silent message, Matthew opted for distraction. Better to avoid labelling their relationship, one way or the other.

"What's in the box, Mrs. Nesbitt?"

Betty's head dropped down at his question. The white paper box tucked under her arm had been all but forgotten amid the excitement. "Oh, that's right," she began, taking a brief moment to compose herself. "Well, I was thinking that since you wouldn't be here at our decorating party this weekend, perhaps you could hang the first ornament on our tree right now."

"Wow," Penny said in wonder, with a low whistle added for good measure. "That's a big honor."

"We all have personalized ornaments," Betty went on, opening the box to reveal a shiny red glass-blown ornament. "And I thought you could help me with this one."

Matthew squinted to read the name spelled in decorative white script.

Daniel. Betty's late husband.

"Oh, Nana," Penny breathed. "That's so sweet of you."

"I'd be honored." Matthew set aside the blanket to rise and graciously accept the ornament. "Where would you like it?"

"Anywhere you like." Betty beamed, the ambient lighting accentuating the moisture in her eyes.

Matthew nodded, then turned toward the tree. Spying a sturdy branch near the top, he reached up high and hung the ornament. As he did, he heard another click from behind his back.

"Nana," Penny laughed. "If you're going to sneak pictures of people, you really should set your phone to silent."

"Who's sneaking?" Betty teased her granddaughter. "It's not my fault if you were too *distracted* to hear me coming."

Matthew grinned. Betty sure was something. Subtle was not it.

"What do you think?" Matthew drew their attention back to the tree.

Betty let out a wistful sigh as she regarded his handiwork. "I think it's just perfect."

From her seat on the couch, Penny nodded. "Me, too."

Drawing his gaze from the tree to the warm glow on the faces of Penny and her grandmother, Matthew felt a contentment he hadn't experienced in a long while. He knew that Betty was just being polite, rewarding him for the visit and the coffee, but being a part of their holiday tradition made it feel like he was part of their family. And that felt really, really good.

"Yeah," he echoed softly, pushing the words past an unexpected lump in his throat. "Me, three."

"So?" Andrew asked expectantly. "What's the verdict?"

Penny took a bite of gingerbread and carefully considered its taste.

"Nope," she repeated glumly. "It's still not the same."

"Bummer." Andrew snapped off a piece and sampled their latest attempt for himself. "You're right," he agreed after a moment. "I guess white peppercorns aren't Nana's secret ingredient."

"Neither are black peppercorns," Penny added. "Or cardamom, or cumin, for that matter."

"Clearly, this is going to be much harder than we thought." Andrew leaned his arms on the large worktable, eyeing the assortment of ingredients as though willing one to confess by the sheer intensity of his gaze. "What else can we try?"

"I'm not sure." She shrugged, wondering if this was truly the best use of their limited prep time before the contest. The siblings had been baking for hours and were no closer to discovering the mystery ingredient than when they began.

"Then it seems like we're fresh out of ideas."

Andrew's dismal announcement brought Penny back to the present. She may have an ulterior motive for participating in the contest, but her primary motivation was always to be the supportive older sister Andrew had missed out on during her time away. If uncovering Nana's secret was that important to him, she wouldn't protest.

Penny reached for a glass of water and took a sip, then broke a small piece off the gingerbread man they had covertly snuck away from Nana's edible army.

"Do Nana's cookies seem…chewier to you?" she asked.

"Maybe a little." Andrew frowned. "But not by much. The texture is almost identical."

Penny nodded, but she wasn't convinced that dismissing the difference was a wise idea. Small details like that could add up to big results.

"It's got to be an extra spice," Andrew concluded, straightening to cross his arms. "But I can't taste anything in there other than cloves, nutmeg, and cinnamon."

"And ginger, of course," Penny added.

"Yeah, naturally." Andrew tapped an impatient finger against his lips, deep in thought. "Nana's cookies taste… sharper, somehow. They've got more of a kick than ours, but it's also subtle. How does she do it?"

"I don't know, but we've already tried four different recipes this morning, so I think it's time we take a break."

Andrew sighed. "I think you're right. Besides that, we now

have the problem of figuring out what to do with all this excess gingerbread."

"I've been thinking about that, too," Penny interjected. "That's why I chose to cut out squares and rectangles instead of the typical gingerbread man shape."

Andrew's eyebrow rose in silent question. "Go on."

"What if we sold pre-made gingerbread house kits online?" she suggested. "That way, people who don't have the time to bake themselves can have the best of both worlds. Homemade gingerbread, all ready to go."

Andrew tilted his head as he listened, a sure sign of his skepticism. "You really think all this online stuff you're working on is going to pay off? I mean, why would somebody in Nebraska or Ohio want to buy cookies from our shop when they could just as easily go to a bakery in their own town?"

"Like I've said, it's all about marketing," Penny reminded him. "Our social strategy is beginning to pay off. We've got almost ten thousand followers, now."

Andrew shook his head. "Those are just numbers right now. We don't know if anybody is invested enough to support us through sales."

"We also don't know if they aren't," Penny countered. "And we won't until we try. Come on, Andy, what have we got to lose?"

"Okay," Andrew shrugged. "If you feel so strongly about it, I won't stop you. Anything to move the five pounds of gingerbread we've baked so far."

Penny chuckled at his attempted humor. "I'm sure our hard work will pay off eventually."

"I hope so."

His eyes were clouded over, but a moment was all it took was for them to alight with the excitement of a new idea.

"Hey, you know what we need?" Andrew asked, mischief causing his lips to part in a wicked grin.

"To hook Nana up to a lie detector?"

"No-o-o." Andrew drew out the word to heighten the anticipation. "Although let's call that plan B." Penny laughed in response to his accompanying wink, but stopped short when he announced, "It's time for a five-minute freak-out!"

An invention of their mother's, intended to release the two rambunctious siblings' pent-up energy, five-minute freak-outs gave Penny and Andrew permission to run, jump, dance, and shout to their hearts' content. For the duration of two songs, one selected by each sibling, anything was fair game. The ritual was a whole lot of fun, but it was also exhausting.

"I don't know about that…" she hemmed.

On one hand, these kinds of silly sibling moments were exactly what she'd missed during her time away, and having a little fun with her brother sounded absolutely incredible. But on the other, how could she join an impromptu dance party without overtaxing her heart? It had already been given the workout of a lifetime being so close to Matthew last night.

"Pick a song." Andrew jogged over to the speaker perched on a shelf on the back wall and pressed the power button with a flourish.

"'Carol of the Bells'?" she offered, vainly hoping that he'd settle for a tamer tune this time.

The suggestion earned her an unimpressed eye roll. "Really, Pinkie?"

"We could use the rock version," she proposed, flashing a weak smile.

Andrew didn't take the bait. "Wow, this is worse than I thought." He turned to the stereo. "I guess I'm choosing first. We need to reprogram you and *fast*. Brace yourself—we're about to go back in time!"

Despite his warning, the sudden blast of music that sounded was so loud, Penny nearly jumped out of her skin.

So much for keeping her heart rate down.

Andrew laughed as he ran back to grab her hands and twirl her around for a beat before releasing her on a spin.

"Come on, Penny!" he exhorted, leaving her to grab a nearby spatula and play air guitar with the upbeat rock song blaring overhead.

Air guitar! The perfect solution to her dilemma. She could easily join in the fun without working up too much of a sweat. Or raising Andrew's suspicions.

Penny reached for a whisk and positioned the tool to play alongside her brother. But despite her best intentions, she felt more embarrassed than entertained. When was the last time she did anything just for the fun of it? She honestly couldn't remember.

"Maybe we should do the robot instead," Andrew yelled close to her ear. "Because you are *stiff*."

"Is that a challenge?" she retorted, the familiar thrum of good-natured indignation beginning to flow through her veins.

"Not hardly," he responded, the teasing glint in his gaze softening the jab. "Wouldn't be any kind of a contest with those lame moves of yours."

"Okay, ," Penny countered, throwing caution to the wind. "You're on."

It didn't take long for the music to get under her skin, and in the mayhem that followed, Penny clapped, jumped, shimmied, and strummed until she forgot all about the contest, the house, and even her heart condition.

Well, almost. That worry was a bit harder to ignore than the rest. But Andrew was right. This boisterous family ritual was exactly what she needed. For the first time in a long time, she felt carefree. Silly.

Alive.

One last power chord, and a frantic jumble of dance moves from Andrew, and the two dissolved into an uncontrollable fit of giggles.

Andrew raised a hand for a high five on a celebratory whoop. "That was awesome!"

Still doubled over by her laughter, Penny barely managed to tap her hand against his.

"That—" she was finally able to breathe, and as she swiped a few joyous tears away from her eyes "—was a great idea."

Her heart was slamming against her chest, and she felt a *lot* dizzier than she should, but Penny stood by her statement. The symptoms would pass soon enough. Making new memories with Andrew was far more important.

Once she cleared up her blurred vision, however, any remaining laughter died in her throat.

"Matthew?" Horror struck as Penny saw the handsome contractor and his sister waiting in the doorframe. "How long have you been standing there?"

"Not very long," he replied, the dimple in his cheek slowly reappearing. "But long enough."

Penny's first instinct was to make an excuse and flee to another room. She fought hard against it and just barely eked out a victory.

How embarrassing!

In stark contrast to her mortification, Andrew seemed invigorated by the surprise audience. "Hey, you guys should join in! Grab a whisk and I'll play Penny's pick, assuming she makes a real choice this time"

"I don't know if that's the best idea," Penny quickly interjected, sending a pointed glance in his direction. One unexpected cardio session had been enough for that morning. She wasn't sure her heart could take another, especially with Matthew as a dance partner.

Andrew met her gaze, a challenge flashing in his eyes. Penny narrowed hers in return.

He waited just long enough to make her sweat, then reneged, reverting to his typical nonchalance with a casual shrug. "Fine, whatever." Turning his attention to the interlopers, he asked, "So what can we do for you?"

"Two things," Cassandra announced. "One, I want to discuss your plan for the grand opening."

As the cochair of the Returning Residents committee, Cassandra had a hand in all the events related to the launch of Mayor Bennett's revitalization project. It was a role that fit her like a glove.

"And two," she continued, clasping her hands together in anticipation as she trained her chocolatey gaze on Penny, "the sinks for the salon came in and I am just *dying* to show you!"

Despite the erratic pounding in her chest, Penny couldn't keep a smile from spreading across her face. Cassandra's enthusiasm, though wildly disproportionate for an event as mundane as a sink delivery, was contagious.

"So what are you?" Andrew nodded in Matthew's direction. "The bodyguard?"

"Andrew!" Penny admonished.

"What?" he said, balking. "It was a joke!"

Matthew's throaty chuckle reassured them both. "Nope. I'm the overworked contractor in serious need of a break."

"How about a cookie?" Andrew offered, reaching for a piece of gingerbread.

"Oh, now you've done it," Cassandra joked. "Better hide the rest or you won't have any left to sell."

"I wouldn't make fun of your work force if I were you," Matthew chided, sinking his teeth into a cookie. "Those fancy sinks of yours could end up installed in the foyer."

"You wouldn't."

"Try me."

"It's okay." Penny stepped in, reaching for another cookie while taking the opportunity to lean against the worktable for support. "We've got lots."

"In that case..." Matthew stepped closer and plucked the gingerbread from her hand. "Don't mind if I do."

His gaze held a playful glint as he looked down at her and took a bite. The dizziness was back, but this time it had nothing to do with her heart condition.

"We're fine-tuning our recipe," Andrew explained, making no mention of the contest.

"That's a lot of fine-tuning," Cassandra observed, taking in the pile of gingerbread cookies behind him. "I hope you'll still have time to work on your display."

Her statement held a question, which Andrew quickly put to rest.

"Of course!" he exclaimed, appalled that she'd even entertain the contrary. "I've got it all figured out. Come on, let me show you the sketches."

With that, Andrew headed toward the small back room that doubled as his office.

"Right behind you," Cassandra replied, looking more than a little pleased as she threw a conspicuous glance in Penny and Matthew's direction.

"Siblings," Matthew scoffed, once she was out of earshot. "Am I right?"

Penny laughed. "Oh, come on, you would be miserable without her."

He looked as though he was about to argue, then thought better of it and shrugged. "Yeah, you're probably right."

Penny noticed he didn't attempt to back away after his cookie snatching, a fact that both excited and unnerved her. "I know I am."

Matthew paused at that statement. Throwing a sidelong glance toward the office, he leaned in even closer. "So how are things going with you and Andrew? It seems like you two are getting along well."

That low voice of his was enough to throw her off balance

all over again. Never mind the fact that he was so close she could feel his breath on her cheeks.

"It's going better than expected," she revealed, pushing the words through a suddenly dry throat. She paused. Frowned. Tried to think over the commotion that her heartbeat was making throbbing in her ears. "Actually, he hasn't mentioned my leaving once. It's like it never happened."

Matthew leaned back slightly to consider her. One eyebrow lifted in question as he did. "And you think that's a bad thing?"

"I don't know," Penny hedged, sneaking another glance at her brother, who was talking animatedly behind his desk. "I guess I'm just wondering if that's not a little strange."

"I wouldn't borrow trouble," Matthew advised on a shrug. "He's probably over it by now."

"You think so?" Penny's eyes flicked back to Matthew, now carefully studying his every move.

"It's not unreasonable. It was a long time ago, after all."

Try as she might, Penny couldn't find a tell. His every last feature stayed perfectly still, from the tip of his forehead all the way down to his chiseled jaw.

"Are you over it?"

The question slipped out before she could think the better of it. Not that she could think clearly at this point, between her symptoms flaring up and Matthew's maddening proximity.

Suddenly shy, he shoved his hands in his pockets and rocked back on his heels. "Well..."

His words were cut off by a ringtone, which sounded far too cheery for the unexpectedly heightened moment. Penny jumped, then looked at the phone resting on the table.

It was Morgan.

"Go ahead." Matthew nodded to the device. "It might be important."

Disappointment settled over her at his suggestion. Clearly,

Matthew was nowhere near interested in answering her question. Was that a bad sign?

Penny gave herself a swift mental kick. What right did she have to look for signs when she was struggling just to stand upright? Hadn't she learned anything with Nick?

Meanwhile, Matthew kept walking and the phone kept ringing. Frustrated, she reached for the device.

"Hello?" The word sounded harsher than she intended.

"Hey, is this a bad time?"

"No, no, I'm sorry," Penny insisted. It wouldn't help anything to unleash her disappointment on her unsuspecting friend. It wasn't her fault that Penny was in this mess, after all. "What's up?"

"I, uh, just wanted to know when you'll be home."

"When I'm home?" she asked. Had Morgan arrived early and unannounced? "Morgan, what's wrong?"

Her question was met with silence. Penny pulled the phone away from her ear to look at the screen. The call hadn't dropped. From across the bakery, she noticed Matthew watching her, a slight frown creasing his lips. She was just about to repeat herself when Morgan found her voice.

"I'm outside on the bench," her friend answered, but the tremor in her voice spoke volumes.

"I'll be right there."

Penny hung up and pushed off the table, praying for the strength to drive home.

Matthew was at her side in an instant. "Everything okay?"

"No, Morgan's back early and I think something's wrong."

"Need a ride?"

Hope filled her heart at his innocent question. Had God just answered her prayer?

"Yes," she breathed, feeling tiny pinpricks threatening at the back of her eyes. "Thank you."

"Hey..." His hand was on her arm, his touch gentle and reassuring. "Everything's going to be okay. I promise."

Penny could only manage a nod as his face began to blur. He meant well, she knew he did. That was just Matthew being his usual gallant self, springing to her rescue like old times. Only they weren't in high school anymore, and her problems were larger than he could possibly imagine, much less handle.

A lead weight tried to settle over her heart, and she tried just as hard to shake it off. Deep down, somewhere beneath the wrestling match, Penny still felt that small glimmer of hope. She wanted to trust in his words. Really, she did.

But she had a sinking feeling that this was one promise Matthew wouldn't be able to keep.

Matthew stole a covert glance in Penny's direction. She hadn't stopped wringing her hands since she'd gotten into the passenger seat of his truck, and her expression was far away and worried.

"So Morgan came home early."

"Yes."

"And that's what's worrying you?"

"Kind of."

Matthew didn't bother concealing his gaze this time. He simply turned his head. The movement seemed to snap Penny out of her reverie.

"Sorry."

"For what?" Matthew replied. "Don't apologize. You did nothing wrong."

He refocused on the road and tightened his grip on the steering wheel.

"I'm sorry for asking. It's none of my business."

When Penny didn't respond, Matthew grit his teeth. Somewhere deep down, he had been hoping for a rebuttal that hadn't come. Hoping that she would tell him she appreciated his looking out for her. Hoping that her answer would...

What? Confirm that she still cared about him, like he did for her?

Why was he asking her these questions? Why did he offer to drive her home? Why did it matter if she chose to confide in him or not?

He knew the answer. If he was honest with himself, Matthew knew that he could never resist playing hero to Penny's damsel in distress. He loved coming to her rescue. Always had. There was a vulnerability about her that brought out his protective instincts, drawing him as inevitably as a moth to a flame.

But how could he make sure he didn't get burned?

Of course, Matthew knew full well that Penny wasn't his responsibility. That she was a grown woman entirely capable of taking care of herself. But when he'd seen that shaken expression on her face, that knowledge had flown away faster than Santa's reindeer.

He stifled a sigh. Was it so wrong of him to want to come to Penny's rescue? To be her hero?

No, he thought, except for one glaring problem.

Penny wasn't a damsel in distress. She didn't need him now any more than she had when they were kids. When life got hard, she'd found her own solution.

It hadn't included him,

Are you over it?

Matthew fought the urge to scoff.

No, he realized indignantly, he was not. Not hardly.

What he was, was in trouble. Because the more time he spent with Penny, the easier it became to fall for her.

A shiver of guilt passed through him.

That wasn't where his focus should be right now. Matthew had more important things to worry about. Like getting her ready for the contest. Like his still unfinished project to honor Mac. That was why he had agreed to partner with Penny in the first place, and it was also why he would see this thing through to the end, no matter what the risk.

Matthew fought hard against a surge of self-doubt. Could he handle spending that much more time with Penny? Especially now that he'd begun to hope for a second chance with her? Honestly, he wasn't so sure.

What Matthew had to remember was that regardless of how well he and Penny had been getting along thus far, their agreement was only temporary. Whether he liked it or not, once they'd accomplished their respective goals, he'd have to let her go.

Again.

Chapter Seven

Penny found Morgan on the bench by Nana's front door just as she said, a large black suitcase resting on the ground beside her. Penny had been nervous on the ride over, but her fears escalated when she saw the blank expression on her friend's face. Staring out at the snow-covered lawn, Morgan looked fragile, as though she'd just returned from a war.

Or, Penny realized with an unpleasant twist in her gut, from a long and drawn-out battle that had finally gotten the best of her.

And where had Penny been that whole time? Climbing the corporate ladder and trying to make a name for herself, logging countless hours while barely taking enough time to sustain herself with overpriced takeout, much less have a real conversation with her family and friends.

Penny had harbored suspicions that Morgan's relationship might not have been going well over the last few months, but she hadn't said a word about it. She'd simply sent a few texts every now and again, telling herself that she was being a good friend by reaching out to Morgan. In theory, she had checked in on her friend, but in practice, she had taken yet another shortcut in life, in order to prioritize other, less important, things.

Like work.

Like her social life.

Like Nick.

Penny felt disgusted with herself. First Nana, and now Morgan. Like a female Ebenezer Scrooge, Penny was beginning to realize just how selfish a life she'd been living up until now.

But just because she had made mistakes in her past didn't mean that it was too late to make things right in the present.

"Hey," she said softly, taking a seat beside Morgan on the bench.

"Hey." Morgan's voice was low. She sounded tired. When she didn't continue, Penny reached over and covered Morgan's hand with hers. It was ice-cold. Morgan gripped her hand like a lifeline, and for a while, the two girls just sat in silence, enfolded by the perfect stillness that only winter could provide.

"You were right," Morgan finally said.

"About what?"

"About Brendan." Morgan's head dipped. She studied the tops of her winter boots. "He was the problem. I just didn't want to believe it." Shifting in her seat, Morgan pulled her cell phone out of her jacket pocket and swiped at the screen. "Things had felt strained for the last few months," she said on a weary sigh. "At least now I know why."

Penny took the phone Morgan offered, then gasped once she saw the image on the screen. A photo of Morgan's boyfriend of three years kissing another woman.

"Brendan had been spending a lot of time at the office," Morgan explained. "After a while, I got suspicious, but he told me I had nothing to worry about. Still, I had this feeling in my gut that something wasn't right, so one night, I stopped by on my way home from work. And this is what I found."

"Oh, Morgan," Penny breathed. "This is terrible! I don't know what to say. I'm so sorry."

Morgan tightened her grip on Penny's hand as fresh tears filled her red-rimmed eyes.

"I just feel so *stupid*," she said, spitting out the words. "I *knew* that something was off, but I trusted him because he asked me to. I even put off coming back because I was waiting for him to say he'd join me. How could I have been so blind?"

"You're not stupid," Penny responded. She wrapped an arm around Morgan's shoulder and pulled her close. "You're a beautiful person, inside and out."

Whether it was the hug or her words, Penny didn't know, but the usually composed Morgan burst into tears, her body shaking against Penny's slight frame. Penny held on tight, sympathizing but saying nothing. Only when her best friend had calmed down did Penny's sorrow turn to indignation.

"You deserve so much better, Morgan," Penny insisted. "Brendan is a grade-A jerk."

Morgan wiped trembling hands across her face. "You can say that again."

Penny's heart broke for her friend. Experiencing betrayal after three months had been bad enough. She could only imagine what three years must feel like.

"I should have been there for you earlier," Penny conceded. "I'm sorry for being such a terrible friend."

"What?" The old Morgan stirred to life then. "How could you even say that, Penny? You're a great friend and always have been."

"Am I? Why didn't I call you instead of texting? Why didn't I visit more often? I could have been there for you, but I wasn't."

"Don't be so hard on yourself," Morgan chided. "I'm the one who kept this hidden. You're not a mind reader."

"I just wish I could have done something to help," Penny replied. "Or that we could have talked about this sooner. I was always so busy. I should have made more time for you."

"It wouldn't have changed anything if you had," Morgan reassured her.

Maybe not, but that didn't prevent Penny from wishing that she could go back and do things differently.

She supposed she should be grateful that she was finally seeing the truth. But would she have time enough to change and live life differently? Or would her heart condition take that opportunity away from her?

"How about we go inside," Morgan suggested. "It's freezing out here."

"Why didn't you use the key?" Penny asked, referring to the spare key tucked under the welcome mat.

"I tried, but I couldn't find it," Morgan answered.

"Really?"

"Yeah, but I did find a lockbox."

"What?" Penny jumped up from the bench and turned toward the door. It was true. She had been so focused on Morgan, she hadn't noticed it when she arrived, but there on the door handle hung a black lockbox, looking entirely out of place against the sage-green door and white frame. Penny rubbed a hand across her forehead. "This can't be happening."

"You didn't know she was selling?" Morgan was beside her now, the suitcase close behind.

"No," Penny groaned. "I found out as soon as I got back."

"Ouch," Morgan replied, her eyebrows creating a furrow in her forehead as they drew close. "That's rough."

"I'll say."

After a beat, Morgan continued. "I would ask how you feel, but it's pretty obvious."

Penny sighed. "It's taken me so long to come home. Now that I'm here, it just seems cruel that my time is so limited."

"I get it," Morgan said, her voice soft. "There are a lot of memories here. But there are also a lot of memories here."

She tapped at Penny's chest, over the place where her heart was struggling to beat.

Penny grew quiet at her friend's reminder. Morgan knew

better than anyone what kind of deep wounds losing a mother could cause.

"I know, I'm being silly," Penny acknowledged, digging for her key inside her purse. "I'm just going to try to ignore it. No sense in ruining our last Christmas here, right?"

A hand on her shoulder stopped Penny in her tracks.

"It's okay to grieve, you know. You listened to my story. I'm here for you, too."

Penny felt her shoulders relax. It suddenly seemed as if all her energy had been spent. "I know," she said, reading concern on her friend's face and wanting to erase it. "But I'm fine. It's just a house. I'll live."

Morgan tilted her head and nailed Penny with a disbelieving look. "Would you have believed me if I had said that about my breakup?"

Penny couldn't argue with her, there. "No."

"So why hide the truth about how you're feeling?" Morgan admonished. "You're in a tough spot, too. Let me help you."

"But you've already been through so much," Penny insisted.

"Maybe so," Morgan agreed. "But I still want to share your burden like you're sharing mine. What does the Bible say about friendship?"

"Um…" Penny vaguely remembered a couple of verses from her brief time spent in the church youth group, but she was pretty sure that John 3:16 wasn't the verse Morgan had in mind.

"Oh, dear, this *is* bad." Morgan's expression turned to one of sympathy. "It says in Ecclesiastes that two are better than one because if one falls, the other will pick him up. Well, I'm here now, and I want to pick you up. Will you let me?"

If Penny was going to open up to Morgan, she had one condition. It would have to be in her room, while seated side-by-side on the floor and resting their backs against the door. The girls had taken up this makeshift barricade on more than one occasion during their time spent growing up together. More often than not, with a tub of ice cream in between them. Why should today be the exception?

"What?" Morgan leaned back against the closed door, her own troubles momentarily forgotten as her spoon pointed upward and hovered over the tub of mint-chocolate ice cream the girls were sharing. "Are you serious?"

"Afraid so." Penny reached for the tub and dug her spoon in deep, searching out the vein of fudge that ran through it. Life was tough. Ice cream helped a lot.

"I can't believe this," Morgan breathed.

"I couldn't, either, at first," Penny revealed. "But believe it. It's true."

"How long have you known?"

"Almost a month, now."

Morgan raised her other hand to her forehead, stunned and, for the first time in recorded history, speechless. "I... I can't even right now."

In spite of the somber topic, Penny had to laugh. "Yeah, well, you've been through a lot, yourself." Stopping the spoon midway to her mouth, she frowned as an unpleasant thought occurred to her. "Was this too much? Did I overshare?"

"No!" Morgan's emphatic response chased away the last of Penny's misgivings. "Not at all! What makes you say that?"

Penny hesitated for just a moment before telling the rest of her story.

"Because that's the reason Nick dumped me."

"What?" Morgan gasped, eyes wide and mouth wider. "Are you kidding me?"

"Nope."

"He left you because you told him about your heart condition?"

"Yep."

Slowly, Morgan began to shake her head. "No. I just... I can't."

"I couldn't, either," Penny repeated. "But once again, it's true."

"Penny..." Morgan turned from her seat on the floor to face her friend, her expression the perfect picture of incredulity. "How are you so calm about this? You find out you're sick, your boyfriend acts like a pile of pond scum, and—and..."

"Don't forget about Nana's house," Penny added.

"Yes, and *that*!" Morgan dropped her spoon into the tub, where it landed with a muted thud. Reaching for her hand, Morgan gave it a good squeeze. "Penny, you have been through so much!"

Penny abandoned her spoon as well and reached for Morgan's other hand. "But so have you."

Morgan's lips flattened as she blew out a long breath. "Fair enough. This fresh start could not have come at a better time, for either of us."

"Here, here," Penny agreed, "And as for being calm... I'm not. Honestly, I'm terrified."

"I can only imagine." Morgan's eyebrows pinched together over worried eyes, deep in thought. "That's a heavy burden to be carrying."

Penny's sentiments exactly.

"But is it all bad news?" her friend asked. "I mean, isn't there some kind of treatment you can have?"

"Yes," Penny admitted. "There's a surgery that's supposed to help. I've been scheduled to have the procedure the first week of January."

Penny had felt a curious mixture of relief and trepidation at the confirmation call she'd received a few nights ago. While not a guarantee, the surgery would at least help the doctors to see exactly what was going on with her heart. And after that... Penny supposed she would have to wait and see.

Just three more weeks. Surely, she could last until then.

"It's still really scary," she continued, her gaze passing over the melting ice cream to study the grooves in the hardwood floor. "And keeping this a secret has been a lot harder than I thought it would be."

"You mean you haven't told anyone?" Morgan gaped. "Not even Nana?"

"No." Penny's answer was immediate. "I can't. Not after what happened with Nick."

"Wait a minute." Morgan blinked fast, a sure sign that she was struggling to process what Penny had told her. "Are you really telling me that because of one jerky guy, you're going to torture yourself by bearing this burden alone instead of letting the people who love you…love you?"

Penny considered her friend's words. "Okay, I guess it does sound kind of ridiculous when you say it like that."

"Ya think?"

"But it's not that easy, Morgan," Penny insisted. "What if Nick was right? What if everyone else freaks out, too? I don't want my family acting weird around me. Or worse, avoiding me."

Which was to say nothing of a certain kindhearted contractor she could mention.

Penny barely had a chance to catch her breath before Morgan's eyes lit up with understanding.

"Hold on!" she exclaimed. "This is why you think you can't be with Matthew, isn't it?"

"Morgan—"

"No, don't you *Morgan* me!" she retorted, waving a hand to erase Penny's weak protest. "You're keeping him at arm's length because of Nick, aren't you? Because of how he reacted to your heart condition, right?"

Penny opened her mouth to protest, but she couldn't lie to her best friend. "Yes."

"Penny!"

"Okay, yes, Nick may have been a jerk, but he had a point," Penny insisted. "I mean, it really wouldn't be fair of me to get involved with someone if there's a chance that I might…"

She tried to finish her sentence. But the words just wouldn't come.

"Penny, no." Morgan pushed the tub of ice cream away from between them and came closer. "Matthew isn't like that. He'll understand."

"But what if he doesn't?" A hard lump started to form in her throat at the thought. "What if…" She tried to form a response, but none came. Wordlessly, Morgan enveloped her in a comforting hug.

"I just can't do it," Penny whispered. "Please don't tell anyone."

Morgan sighed, and for a moment, Penny thought she might protest.

"I won't," Morgan agreed quietly. "I may disagree with your decision, but if you're not ready to share, then we'll just keep this between us. We've gotten through worse before. We can handle it. With God, all things are possible."

Penny leaned back to study her friend. The Morgan she remembered hadn't been so grounded in her faith.

"It sounds like you've been reading your Bible."

"It sounds like you haven't," Morgan countered.

Penny nodded, her lips a grim line. "You'd be right about that."

In the wake of her mother's death, Penny had initially tried to find solace in Scripture, but it had been hard. Separated from her family and church community, Penny quickly gave up, taking the easy way out and allowing anger and resentment to get the better of her. Instead of turning toward God, she'd turned away. Instead of relying on Him, she'd put her trust in herself. And now, so much time had passed that she wasn't sure she even knew how to find her way back.

"It's never too late to start." Morgan seemed to read Penny's thoughts. "How about we pray together?"

For the second time that day, hope flickered to life deep inside Penny's heart. She may have forgotten about God, but was it possible He hadn't forgotten about her? She wasn't sure, but she felt ready to find out.

"That sounds great."

Evening found Matthew driving a familiar route into the heart of Cedar Ridge, first down Main Street, then left on Fifth, then through to the end, where Mrs. Nesbitt's Colonial stood as tall and as proud as the day it had been built. The drive had been an impulsive decision on his part, and it had him thinking back to a time when he wouldn't have thought twice about knocking on the door and inviting Penny out for the evening. Talking, tailgating, stargazing... He smiled as the memories came rushing back. Those were some great times.

Could he really be faulted for wanting to have more?

As Matthew turned into the driveway, he noticed the porch lights were off, but there were a few interior lights shining through second-floor windows. Good. At least someone was home. After spending the last couple of days trying to forget how badly he was missing Penny, he would have hated to miss her again tonight.

Matthew killed the engine and hopped out, not bothering to lock the vehicle. He wouldn't be long. At least, that's what he told himself.

The spring in his step was a potent reminder of just how easy it would be for him to slip back into old habits, old friendships, and, yes, old feelings.

Not that the feelings he was experiencing now were the same as they had been in adolescence. They had both grown a lot since then. He into a quiet mountain man, and she into a polished businesswoman. Matthew chuckled at the contrast. What a pair they made. And yet, even though their paths had taken them in very different directions, the connection between them still felt as tangible and as powerful as ever.

Even more so.

Their bond may be built on the foundation of their teenage friendship, but it was so much more than that. Somehow, despite their distance, it seemed as if that bond had matured right alongside them. Whatever draw he may have initially felt toward Penny was nothing compared to the irresistible force that stirred to life whenever he was around her now.

But, he quickly reminded himself, Matthew had to keep his priorities straight, for both their sakes. True, he was finding himself less and less opposed to the idea of a Christmas romance with each passing day. But first things first—he had to get to the bottom of her return to Cedar Ridge and find out if she really intended to stay.

The sound of snow crunching underneath his boots created a steady rhythm as he walked. It was a crisp winter night, and the sky was clear. It called his attention from the snow to the full moon and brightly lit stars.

"Fancy seeing you here."

Matthew nearly jumped out of his skin when the greeting broke into his thoughts. Gathering his wits, he refocused to find Penny curled up under a blanket on the porch bench.

"Man, you sure know how to get a guy's heart racing."

She rewarded him with a sweet laugh. "I'm sure you say that to all the girls."

"Only the ones who scare the living daylights out of me," he countered, stepping onto the porch. "What are you doing out here, anyway?"

"I could ask you the same question," she pointed out, an impish glint dancing in her eyes.

He couldn't conceal a smile. "I asked you first."

Another laugh followed, then an invitation to join her on the bench.

"I could tell you," she began, gathering the blanket so he could take a seat. "But it looks like you've already figured out the answer." She pointed toward the winter sky. "The stars are beautiful tonight."

As he eased himself onto the bench beside her, Matthew was careful to keep a safer distance between them this time. Once he was settled in, she offered him the blanket to share.

"Do you remember the time we went stargazing?" she asked, innocently enough.

He bit back a laugh.

"How could I forget?" he replied. "You knew the name of every last constellation out there. And then some."

Penny chuckled. "Yes, well, I learned all that from my mom." She turned her gaze out toward the luminaries dotting the evening sky, a relaxed smile gracing her delicate lips. "We used to sit out here for hours, drinking hot chocolate and staring at the stars."

"That sounds nice."

"It was." The corners of her lips dropped slightly, mimicking the dip in her voice. "I mean, it still is. I just haven't done this in a while, that's all."

Matthew nodded, understanding her dilemma all too well.

"Do you feel closer to her out here?" he asked after a beat.

"Kind of." Penny smoothed a hand over the blanket as she thought. "This was our special time together. Andrew could never handle the cold, with or without the hot chocolate, so it was always just me and Mom. She would make up her own constellations to entertain me. One year for my birthday, she even named a star after me."

Matthew raised an eyebrow in surprise. "You can do that?"

"Apparently." She grinned. "It was the best present ever.

It's somewhere over there." She pointed to a cluster of stars to their right. "I used to look at it through our telescope, but I can't find it now. Probably got packed away somewhere."

"Has Betty already started packing?"

"Oh, yes," Penny sighed. "She's leaving the essentials out until after Christmas, of course, but her books, photo albums, and ceramic trinkets are all packed away, along with her summer wardrobe."

"Wow," Matthew whistled. "Sounds like she's been busy."

"She has," Penny confirmed. "I've been helping her too, when I'm not at the bakery. It's been a good way to get reacquainted with her and my mom." She paused, deep in thought. "I guess it's also become a way of saying goodbye."

"The people we love never really leave us, you know," Matthew offered. "They live on in our memories, our habits, and our stories. Your Mom will always be there, inside your heart."

Penny hummed. "That's a nice thought." But she didn't seem convinced.

Matthew's chest tightened at the sadness that laced her words. He decided a topic change was in order.

"How's Morgan doing?" he asked.

"Good." She nodded first, then shrugged. "Well, better now, anyway. The first couple of days were a bit of an adjustment for her, but I think we're both finding our footing."

Once again, Mathew wondered what exactly it was that Penny was struggling with. But he couldn't very well ask her point-blank. Not without scaring her away again. But whatever it was, he hoped that her best friend's return would help.

"Morgan was actually just out here with me, but she ran back inside when we saw your truck pull in."

Matthew chuckled, remembering the countless times he'd caught sight of Morgan's retreating back as she flew away to give him some alone time with her best friend. "Looks like nostalgia is contagious."

Penny hummed an affirmation, an easy smile lingering on her face. "Is that why you came by?" She angled her head to look at him. "Because you were feeling nostalgic?"

"No." He smiled back, altogether too entranced with the way the stars were being reflected in her eyes. "I came because I wanted to see you."

Penny drew in a quick breath, then ducked her head back down. He couldn't tell in the dark, but if he had to guess, he figured her cheeks were probably the color of Rudolph's nose right about now.

"It's been a couple of days," he commented, opting to steer the conversation into more neutral territory. "We had to put up the wallpaper without you. You should have seen Cass and me trying to get the line straight."

Penny laughed, the sound soft and light. "Oh, I can imagine. That must have been quite a struggle."

"Oh, you don't know the half of it," Matthew continued. "But the result was totally worth it. It looks really good."

"I can't wait to see it," Penny said. "And I'm sure Morgan is just as anxious for the big reveal."

"It won't be that much longer now," he reassured her. "There are only a couple things left to do, so we should be able to give Morgan the keys to the salon by the end of the week."

"Wow, that quick, huh?" Penny asked. "You must have hired an amazing contractor."

The teasing glint in her eyes was far too tempting for a friendly conversation. And the warmth in her smile... That had to mean something, didn't it?

"Oh, yeah," he said, playing along. "The best in the business."

Penny's smile wavered, trailing off on a little chuckle. "Speaking of business, I don't want you to think that I've forgotten about my end of the bargain."

"I don't," Matthew replied quickly.

Although truthfully, he hadn't thought about Mac's project in a while. Like an old adversary looking for a rematch, guilt crept up and settled itself firmly on his back at the reminder.

Just when he thought he'd caught a break, too.

Matthew clenched his jaw, bracing as familiar accusations began to rise.

It was your fault he died. This is the absolute least you can do.

"Well, that's very generous of you," Penny continued, her drawn eyebrows creating a tiny furrow above her nose. "But I know we still have a lot of work to do, and not a lot of time to do it. Maybe we can squeeze in an interview sometime this week after training."

"Penny, it's okay." Unthinkingly, Matthew rested a hand on hers to reassure her. "We'll get to it eventually."

And besides, this was his burden to carry, not hers. She had enough on her plate already without him adding to her load.

She tilted her head to the side. "But you're spending so much time helping me. That's not fair to you."

"Even if I'm okay with it?" he countered.

"Especially then." Penny smirked. "You're too generous for your own good, you know that?"

Her words of approval caused his chest to swell. Suddenly, he became very aware of their joined hands, the quiet of the evening, and the rapid pounding of his heart.

He forced himself to lean back and pull away, noticing that it was getting harder to do so each time he did.

"Do me a favor and tell that to Cassandra," he joked, leaning on humor to deflect from the serious turn his thoughts had taken. "I could use a good word with the boss."

"I'm sure she already knows what a hard worker you are."

"Hmm." He stroked his chin, pretending to think deeply about the matter. "Maybe that's why she keeps adding to my never-ending to-do list."

Penny smiled in response, but the softness in her gaze made him suspect she saw right through him.

"So when can I come by to keep working?"

Boom. Right to the chase. No preamble. Matthew was right. He might as well be transparent, as far as Penny was concerned.

"I've got a few things left to do in the salon, but I don't think it'll take all day."

She nodded. "So tomorrow, then?"

"Sure," he agreed. Why not? He wanted to see her just as much as she wanted to help him. It was a win-win. "I'll let you know when I head for home."

"Sounds good."

Matthew mirrored her nod, then pushed aside the blanket, intending to leave. "Guess I'll leave you to it, then."

"Matthew, wait."

He sunk back down and turned to look at her.

"I, uh…" If the waver in her voice hadn't told him she was nervous, the absentminded wringing of her hands would have been a dead giveaway. "I've been thinking a lot about our last conversation."

"Oh?"

"I know this is coming really, *really* late, but… I think I owe you an apology."

"For what?"

"For leaving town without telling you, all those years ago," she continued. "I know it was extremely cowardly of me." She looked at him then, eyes bright and pleading. "But I just couldn't bear the thought of saying goodbye."

Matthew exhaled a breath he hadn't realized he'd been holding. "Penny, it's okay. I'm not mad at you for leaving. Never was." He shrugged. "I mean, I wondered about it, but I could never be mad at you."

She nodded, then gazed down at her hands. "I wanted to call you after I got to New York, you know."

He snapped to attention at that. "You did?"

"Yeah. I kept dialing your number and then immediately hanging up." She released a breathy laugh at the memory. "I even tried writing to you a couple of times, but I could never bring myself to send the letters."

In that moment, Matthew could have been bowled over by a snowflake. He couldn't believe what he was hearing. All this time, he thought she hadn't needed him, but maybe that wasn't the case. Maybe this homecoming really could be their second chance, after all.

"I guess what I'm trying to say is, I didn't forget about you," Penny concluded. "Exactly the opposite."

A smile played at the corners of his mouth. "Even though you didn't try to look me up?"

"Wow, you're not going to let me live that down, are you?"

"Not a chance," he teased.

"Fine," she acknowledged. "I should have tried harder to find your nonexistent social-media profiles. There, are you happy now?"

He had to laugh at the absurdity of her statement. "Well, when you put it that way..."

She smiled. "While we're being honest, you might as well know the reason I didn't try to find you." She drew in a breath, squeezed her eyes shut, then blew it back out. "I was scared that I'd find out you'd become a famous football player and married a supermodel or something."

Matthew burst into laughter. "Man, you've got some imagination."

"It could have happened!" she protested. "You were certainly good enough, and last I heard, you were going to a big-time college on a football scholarship."

"Ah." Right. That hadn't lasted very long. But despite the

dismal turn his football career had taken, Matthew found himself more amused than disappointed with the way his life had turned out after all. "Let's just say, God had other plans for me."

"Really?" One eyebrow raised in a delicate arch. "How so?"

There it was. The invitation to share, to let her into his past. He'd known that it would come eventually, but surprisingly, this time he felt ready to accept. But only on one condition.

"Are you planning to stay in Cedar Ridge long-term?"

Blue eyes widened in surprise. "Where did that come from?"

He shrugged, aiming for casual. "Just curious."

She waited a moment before giving him her answer.

"Yes." The affirmative should have eased his concern. But the time it took for her to decide, paired with the way she shifted in her seat, was hardly convincing. "At least, that's the plan."

"So nothing permanent?"

Penny's eyes seemed to search his soul as she studied him in that silently inquisitive way of hers. He fought hard not to squirm, wondering what she was seeing.

"I may have to go back and forth to New York for a while to settle a few things," she finally admitted. "But my intention is to stay here in Cedar Ridge. Assuming everything works out."

Swing and a miss. Not really the reassuring answer he'd been looking for.

Matthew acknowledged her words with a nod while considering their implications. Everything she said sounded like good news. But the nagging feeling in his gut told him something wasn't right. Too bad Penny wasn't offering any clues as to what that something might be. Other than her troubled expression, that was.

"Tell you what," Matthew offered, abandoning this conversational diversion to return to her initial request. "We can talk more about my story tomorrow, after we work on the website. Okay?"

Penny quirked an eyebrow up in question, as if she wasn't quite sure what to make of his hasty topic changes. But to her credit, she recovered quickly and didn't confront him about them.

"Hmm." Penny tapped a finger to her chin, seeming to consider his proposal. "Well, seeing as how I've been waiting this long already, I suppose an extra day won't hurt."

"Is that your not-so-subtle attempt at guilt?" Matthew asked.

"Maybe," she said slyly. "But only if it's working."

"I'd be careful with the guilt card if I were you." He raised an eyebrow to underscore the warning. "Two can play at that game."

"In that case, I'd better quit while I'm ahead," she giggled.

The sound burrowed deep into his heart and filled it up fast. For what seemed like the billionth time, Matthew was struck by how natural and effortless it felt to be with Penny. It would be so easy to fall in love with her all over again. But for right now, it was best that he retreat for the night and see what he could discover tomorrow. Who knows? Maybe opening up about his past would encourage her to do the same. And if Matthew could get to the bottom of whatever was going on with Penny, well, maybe that Christmas romance wouldn't be so far out of reach after all.

"Good night, Penny." He said, rising to leave.

"Good night, Matthew," she replied. "And…thank you for coming to see me."

The affection shining in her eyes froze the breath in his lungs.

She was beautiful.

"Anytime," he answered, in a voice that sounded raspy to his ears. He cleared his throat, taking the opportunity to step away and hit the reset button. "I hope you have sweet dreams."

He watched as her expression changed. Subtly but surely, contentment turned to…melancholy?

"Thanks," she responded quietly. "I think I will."

Chapter Eight

"How's it coming in here?"

Cassandra's voice rang in Matthew's ears, quickly followed by a boisterous laugh that he recognized as belonging to Gwen Hastings, the second member of the Little Miss Matchmakers, and the only one who hadn't moved away from Cedar Ridge. She and her husband, Robert, ran a quaint bed and breakfast in town.

From his post, crouched low to the ground, Matthew turned to face his visitors.

"Wow, you weren't kidding about that teal theme," she marveled. "Not even the *trim* is immune."

Matthew watched as Gwen's eyes roamed about the almost-completed space. He'd learned a long time ago not to question his sister when it came to her design choices. Or anything, really. Teasing her, however, was still firmly on the table.

"You should see the sinks," he chimed in, gesturing to the teal ceramic installations.

Gwen's hand rose to cover her mouth. "Oh, my."

"And what exactly is wrong with the trim and sinks?" Cassandra challenged playfully, planting a fist on her jutted hip.

"Nothing." Gwen grinned. "It's just a little unconventional, don't you think?"

"And since when have I ever been described as conventional?"

Gwen laughed at her friend's rebuttal. "Fair point."

Matthew simply shook his head and returned to his work, dipping his paintbrush into a can of teal paint.

"But you have to admit," Cassandra said, in lecture mode, from somewhere above his head. "It works brilliantly in the space."

"You know what would work even better?" Matthew asked. "You holding a paintbrush."

Cassandra responded with a slick eyebrow raise. "What's eating you? I thought you'd be more relaxed by now. We're almost done."

"Morgan is back now," he calmly stated. "And she's going to need time to prepare her shop for the grand opening, which, I might remind you, is right around the corner."

An odd twinge in his chest stopped him short. That didn't give him a lot of time to prepare, either. True, he had a lot on his mind recently, but that was no excuse to forget about his plan to unveil Mac's artwork. The truth was, Matthew had been slacking off. And there was no excuse for that.

"Matthew is just a little out of sorts because he hasn't seen Penny in a while," Cassandra exaggeratedly whispered to Gwen.

"Ah," her friend played right along. "I see."

Matthew clenched his jaw. Clearly, his relationship with Penny wasn't progressing as fast as Cassandra would like. He should have known his sister would send for reinforcements eventually.

On the bright side, they were still one member short of completing their unstoppable trifecta. As far as Matthew knew, Riley Jennings was still living in Nevada, and wouldn't be coming back to join forces with her meddlesome friends anytime soon.

"Are you two dating?" Gwen's question was directed at him, although Matthew took great care to avoid making eye contact with her by taking his time carefully swiping another coat of paint onto the trim.

"No."

"I thought you might be," the tall blonde continued. "Seeing as how you were so cute together back in high school. Personally, I always hoped for a happy ending."

"So did I," Cassandra added. "But you know what they say. Better late than never."

Matthew fought the urge to sigh. The last thing he felt like doing was sharing the details of his love life with two-thirds of the notorious Cedar Ridge matchmakers. Unfortunately for him, he was cornered.

"So there *is* a spark?" Gwen insisted.

"I certainly think so," Cassandra affirmed. "But someone isn't telling me the details."

"Maybe *someone* would prefer that you talk to him instead of about him," Matthew said evenly.

He regretted the words as soon as they were out of his mouth. Now he'd really done it. But he had to give the girls credit. He had chosen to ignore them and they'd quickly turned the tables, roping him in despite himself.

"You know, Matthew, Robbie and I lost a lot of time because neither of us knew how the other felt," Gwen advised.

His heart gave a little leap at her seemingly innocent comment. Penny hadn't said as much last night, but it certainly sounded like she cared for him. Or, had cared? But how could he be sure?

"Does that sound familiar?" Gwen asked.

He risked a glance up and found two sets of eyes gleaming with mischief. The sight made him wonder what exactly he had gotten himself into.

"I'm not going to answer that."

Cassandra leaned closer to tell Gwen, "That would be a yes."

Matthew sighed, loud enough that the two friends should have gotten the message. Too bad they weren't interested in heeding it.

"Does she know how he feels?"

"Not yet."

Matthew stood, tired of their games.

"If you have something to say, then just tell me, already," he suggested, eyes darting between his two visitors. "The sooner you do, the sooner I'll be able to finish this trim work."

"Do you remember when I was offered that job in Kentucky?" Gwen asked.

Her question took him by surprise. What did that have to do with him and Penny?

"Yes."

As Matthew recalled, Gwen had been offered a job a few months after she'd graduated college and moved back to Cedar Ridge.

"I was hoping that Robbie would ask me to stay, but days passed and he didn't say anything. That made me think we might just be friends, and that he didn't return my feelings. I was crushed. I would have left without ever knowing that he cared for me, too, if Cassandra and Riley hadn't intervened."

"So what happened?"

Gwen and Cassandra exchanged a look.

"I had packed up and was just about to leave when suddenly, someone started knocking on my door."

"Robert," Matthew supplied.

"Yup," Cassandra picked up the thread. "Riley and I were rooming in Seattle, miles away, but we knew we had to do something. So we drove all the way back here and ended up at Robbie's house. After we barged our way in, we convinced him that he was making a big mistake by not telling Gwen how he felt."

"And let me guess. You want me to do the same thing now, with Penny."

"Well, of course," Gwen confirmed, smiling brightly. "You

didn't tell Penny how you felt the last time you two were together, and look how that ended up."

"Hold on," Matthew held up a hand. "Are you really trying to tell me that it's my fault that Penny left Cedar Ridge the last time?"

"Not your fault, per se," Gwen hedged. "But don't you think she might have stayed if you had told her how you felt?"

The question gave him pause. Matthew hadn't considered that before. But now that he had...

Could Gwen be right? Was Penny waiting for him to reveal his true feelings for her? And if he did, would that be enough to convince her to stay in Cedar Ridge for good?

Matthew shook his head. He wasn't sure what to think when it came to Penny. He hadn't slept well last night, spending the better part of the evening mulling over everything she'd said. Not that it had done him any good. Morning came, and he still hadn't the faintest idea of what could be causing that inexpressible sadness he'd repeatedly glimpsed in her expression. Or what he should do about it. Part of him wanted to relax, to say that it was just his imagination playing tricks with him and leave it at that. But deep down, he knew that wasn't the case. And if there was something else going on with her, he would have to discover what that was before confessing his feelings.

Wouldn't he?

A soft hand on his shoulder caught his attention. Cassandra.

"Just think about it. Okay?"

Matthew nodded in silent agreement. He had a lot to think about, that was for sure.

"Hey, why don't you head out for the day?" Cassandra offered, reaching for his paintbrush. "You've been working really hard these days, and you look like you could use a break. I can finish up here."

Matthew was shocked. Not by his sister's compassion, of course. He knew full well that she hid a generous heart beneath that confident facade. But if she was willing to pause their usual teasing banter to give him some rest, then he must really look a mess. Maybe he could use a break, after all.

Matthew released the brush and gratefully accepted her offer. "Thanks, sis."

"No problem," she reassured him, an impish glint dancing in her eyes. "Can't have you showing up red-eyed and lethargic for Penny's training, after all."

Ah, yes. He should have known. He hadn't breathed a word about his meeting with her later today, but Cassandra didn't need a reason to push. She'd poke and prod him about this until the day he proposed.

"Don't you two ever quit?" he asked, amazed.

Cassandra flashed her thousand-watt smile at him. "You know I don't."

Gwen mirrored her gesture beside her. "Neither do I."

Matthew had to hand it to them, even if begrudgingly. The Little Miss Matchmakers were relentless when it came to their romantic schemes. And now that he and Penny were in their crosshairs, he wouldn't be able to avoid the truth for much longer.

If he put off telling Penny how he felt, Cassandra and Gwen could very well do it for him. At the very least, they wouldn't relent until he made that decision himself.

A part of him wondered if he should be honest with Penny sooner rather than later. He'd have the perfect opportunity later today. He could take the girls' advice and tell Penny that he wanted her to stay. But he couldn't help but worry about how she would respond.

Would honesty guarantee a happy ending, or put it in jeopardy?

There was only one way to find out.

Penny couldn't believe her eyes.

"Andrew, we sold out of our gingerbread-house kits last night. That's over a hundred orders!"

"What?" Andrew's head shot up from where he stood, hunched over a tiny fondant figurine. "You mean a hundred people want to buy our gingerbread-testing leftovers? How did that happen?"

"With the right branding, that's how." Penny beamed. "And they're not leftovers. They're precut homemade gingerbread panels. The perfect combination for great taste and easy assembly."

"Tomato, tomahto," Andrew scoffed. "It's still just gingerbread. You can't tell me that other bakeries aren't doing the same thing."

"No," she replied. "But that's where your engaging personality and my solid social strategy come into play."

Andrew harrumphed. "Social strategy. Just another term for you sitting on your phone while I do all the heavy lifting around here."

"Not so," Penny retorted. "Every one of our orders came from social media."

Andrew quirked up a skeptical eyebrow in question. "Seriously?"

"No joke," she went on, turning the phone to face him. "See for yourself. Sweet Surprises is a hit! You're up to forty thousand followers."

"What?" Squinting at the screen, Andrew was flabbergasted. "It's not even been a month. That's insane!"

"No," Penny countered. "That's strategy."

Too bad Matthew wouldn't let her use that same strategy to draw attention to his artwork. If he did, she might actually stand a chance of holding up her end of their bargain. As it was, she was already dreadfully behind. There was only one week remaining until the cookie contest. That wasn't nearly enough time to oversee an effective marketing campaign.

Unless, of course, they extended their deal a while longer. Matthew had asked about her intention to stay in Cedar Ridge last night. Could it be that he didn't want her to leave? That he might want to move beyond their temporary partnership and into friendship?

Or maybe… more than friendship?

Hope swelled momentarily before reality rose to contain it.

More than friendship was off the table as long as her heart remained compromised. Friendship might even be a step too far.

Penny's stomach turned. She couldn't bear the thought of not seeing him again once the contest was over. But what could she do?

"I guess now the pressure's really on to create a stellar cake."

Andrew's serious tone quickly brought her back down to earth. When she did, she found him laser-focused on the edible sculpture in his hands.

"No pressure," Penny amended. "Just keep on being you. That's what your followers are looking for."

A derisive snort embellished the offending word. "Followers. Makes me sound like some kind of pseudocelebrity."

"No," she insisted. "It makes you sound like an interesting person."

"Whatever." Andrew quickly brushed away that idea, looking uncomfortable. "What do you think?"

He held up the completed figure, a strikingly detailed miniature wise man.

"It's incredible," Penny replied honestly.

"Thanks. One down, two to go. This cake is going to be *epic*."

Penny wrestled with an amused grin and lost. "I don't doubt it."

Nothing was ever ordinary when it came to Andrew. Epic was the name of his game. Case in point, the gigantic five-tier cake he was putting together for the grand opening, which would illustrate the Nativity story.

"I'm thinking we should also have a takeaway item for people to grab," he went on. "Maybe a miniature Nativity cookie?"

"Will you be able to complete that many cookies in time?" Penny asked, concerned. Her brother may be a hard worker, but they were up against a tight deadline, especially factoring in their repeated attempts to uncover the riddle of Nana's secret gingerbread recipe. They were probably better off baking something less intricate.

"Not a chance," he replied breezily. "That's why you're going to decorate them."

"Me?"

"Yeah, you," Andrew insisted, picking up another piece of fondant and working it in his hands. "Your piping work has really been improving over these last couple weeks. I think you're up to the challenge."

Penny wasn't so sure. She was nowhere near as talented as Andrew. And considering she had only acted as his sous chef for these last few weeks, this project would be a huge—and entirely unmerited—jump in responsibility.

What was he up to?

"Thanks," she replied evenly. "But I'm still not close to your level."

"Still, I'm impressed," he declared. "What's your secret?" Andrew threw a quick glance her way, the mischief darting in his pale blue eyes spelling his downfall.

Penny narrowed her eyes. "What do you mean?"

"I mean you've really come a long way, Pinkie," Andrew continued, the edges of his lips giving way to a lopsided grin. "If I didn't know any better, I'd think you were sneaking back in here to practice without me."

"How could you possibly know that?" She gaped at him.

Andrew's grin grew wider as icy blue eyes warmed with mirth. "Did you forget that I set up a security system in here?"

Penny bit back a groan. Now that he mentioned it, she vaguely recalled some talk of installing security cameras during a phone call they had before she agreed to partner. She had waved off the idea as unnecessary, especially in a small town like Cedar Ridge, but it seemed that Andrew had stuck to his original plan.

"If you knew all this time, why didn't you say anything?"

"Wanted to see if I could figure it out for myself." He shrugged, pausing only long enough to poke some good-natured fun at himself. "Wow, first Nana's recipe, now this… The urge to solve mysteries must be contagious."

"You always were partial to the Hardy Boys series," she recalled, hoping to distract him.

"Right. Guess I learned a thing or two." He smirked.

"Remind me to call you if ever I need a private eye."

"Hopefully you never do." After putting down the fondant, Andrew crossed his arms and leaned against the worktable. "So tell me. Why are you baking after hours with Matthew Banks?"

Penny sighed. There was no use in hiding the truth anymore. She might as well come clean.

"He's…training me for the contest."

"Are you kidding?" Andrew leaned forward, eyes now wide enough to match his smile. "You hired a *contractor* to train you for a baking competition? Why didn't you ask me?"

"Because I didn't want you to know how scared I am," Penny admitted.

Dark eyebrows drew close to overshadow his gaze. "You're scared?"

"Yes." The word, once released, left a feeling of relief in its wake. Penny hadn't realized how heavily all these secrets had been weighing on her. "Terrified, actually. But I didn't want to let you down again, so I've been practicing with Matthew." Nervously, she wrung her hands together, trying to discern Andrew's true feelings about the matter. "Are you mad at me?"

"Mad?" he repeated, incredulous. "You're facing your fear for my sake. That's incredible. Why would I be mad?"

That first trickle of relief gave way to a veritable flood, washing over her like a tidal wave.

Andrew wasn't upset. She was so glad!

Although, she quickly noticed, he didn't address that bit about her letting him down before. Did that mean something? Or was she overthinking things?

"Honestly, the thing I'm most upset about is that you've gotten so much better at decorating cookies by working with him instead of me!" Andrew laughed, returning to his sculpture. "That stings."

Freed from her secret, Penny found his laughter to be contagious. "Well, now that you know, I'm happy to transfer all future coaching-related duties to you."

"Oh, we'll definitely put in some extra time," Andrew agreed. "But far be it from me to deprive you of your romantic baking rendezvous."

"My *what*?" Penny's face began to flame. "Andrew, you're being ridiculous!"

"Am I?" He reached over and brushed a finger against her cheek. "Or did you forget why I call you Pinkie?" The heat—and her embarrassment—grew in time with Andrew's smug grin. "By the way," he added, pointing to the spot he'd left behind. "You've got icing sugar on your cheek now."

Penny rubbed a hand against the place, then examined her palm.

Yup. White powder. Meeting his gaze, she saw the challenge in his eyes.

"Okay," she said, tilting her chin up to call his bluff. "Have it your way, then."

Andrew made no move to stop her as she swiped her hand along the icing-dusted worktable. Fully loaded with his weapon of choice, she stared down her brother.

"You ready for this?"

Down went the second wise man. Up went his two powdered hands.

"Oh, it's on."

For what was probably the hundredth time since he'd received her message, Matthew pulled up the picture Penny had sent him on his phone. For the life of him, he couldn't imagine what might have prompted an icing-sugar throwdown, but from the looks of the siblings' postwar selfie, it had been one doozy of a battle.

Might be a little late.

Matthew chuckled anew at the text that came along with the photo. No kidding. It would take more than a little while to clean up that mess. And he wasn't just talking about the white streaks in her hair and on her clothes, either. Between the sugar-dusted tables and floor, it looked as though the kitchen had just weathered a saccharine blizzard.

Not that the veritable snowstorm detracted any from the pure joy radiating from Penny's face. Matthew couldn't help but smile back. She looked so carefree, so relaxed…so different from the guarded woman who had shown up back in town just a few weeks ago. She'd changed a lot in that short time.

So had he, Matthew belatedly realized. Especially considering he was about to open up about the biggest mistake of his life. Matthew had considered Cassandra and Gwen's suggestion to be honest with Penny since leaving Morgan's salon. But before he could do that, he had to come clean about the real reason he was trying so hard to get Mac's art into the world.

Matthew didn't think he'd ever want to share that story. And technically, he still didn't. But he did want Penny to understand the motivation behind this project.

No. That wasn't entirely true, he realized. It mattered much more that Penny understand *him*.

That thought gave him pause. Maybe Cassandra was right. As she so loved to remind him, Matthew had it *bad*.

The crunch of gravel under tires called him back to the present, sending his stomach into a free fall.

"Sorry I'm late," Penny called as she stepped out of the car.

"Can't say I blame you," Matthew replied from his place on the porch, leaning against the railing. Despite his nerves, an easy smile spread across his face at the sight of her. "Looks like you two had a fun day."

"Oh, gosh, the best," she said, practically gushing as she ascended the three steps to where he stood. "Much better than boardroom meetings, that's for sure."

Matthew felt an odd twinge at the thought of Penny in a boardroom, high up in a corporate skyscraper. It didn't seem right. He just couldn't picture Penny cooped in in an office building all day—especially in the middle of a bustling metropolis like New York City. No, he thought, the Penny he knew seemed far more suited to afternoon walks in the woods and leisurely Sunday lunches after church. And stargazing, of course. Preferably with him in tow.

"Are you ready to get started?" she asked, eyes still aglow from her earlier diversion.

"Actually," Matthew began, trying hard to keep from getting lost in those blue-grey depths, "I was thinking it might be better if we talked a little first."

Surprise quickly transformed exuberance into curiosity. "Oh?"

He shifted his weight to steady himself. Matthew told himself that he had no need to worry. He knew her heart, after all.

He knew he'd find compassion, not condemnation. But even so, this was going to be a lot less fun than an icing-sugar war.

"I have a bit of a confession," Matthew said. "I haven't been completely honest with you."

Delicate eyebrows dipped over anxious eyes. "What do you mean?"

Oh, he hated that look on her face. Fear, hurt, and sympathy all rolled into one.

"I haven't made it very easy for you to hold up your end of our deal," Matthew explained. "Because I haven't told you why I'm so passionate about this project."

"Oh." Melancholy laced the obvious relief in that softly spoken word. "It's okay. You don't owe me any explanations."

"I know," he went on. "But I want to tell you, Penny. I want you to...understand."

"Okay." Penny's smile was slight, and it wavered at the edges, but beneath her apprehension, it was genuine. "I'm all ears."

Matthew nodded.

"What do you remember about my dad?"

"Your dad?" she repeated, surprised. "Um, I think he was a broker of some kind? Traveled a lot. Very into football."

Matthew assented with a derisive snort. "That's about right."

"You also told me once that he put a lot of pressure on you," Penny added, her voice subdued.

Matthew's heart softened at the sweetness in her tone. "He did," he replied quietly. "We had very different ideas about how I should live my life. Still do."

"Really?" The cute way she wrinkled her nose called his attention to her adorable smattering of freckles. "I thought you wanted to play football professionally. Or at least, you did back in high school."

"You're right," Matthew admitted. "But I was only walking that path because it was what my dad wanted. When I got to college, things got very real very fast, and I had to face the truth."

Penny leaned against the railing beside him, shrinking the gap between them. "What happened?"

"First, I fell behind in my classes because I was spending too much time on the field. Then I tore my ACL, which took me off the team and nullified my scholarship. Finally, after a brutal round of midterms, I got suspended."

"Oh, my," Penny breathed, resting a comforting hand on his arm. "I'm so sorry that happened to you."

Matthew's immediate instinct was to cover her hand with his, to keep her close. But after the way she reacted the last time, he figured the best course of action was no action at all.

"Don't be," he replied, flicking his gaze down to her hand for a lingering moment before drawing it back up again. "I didn't realize it then, but getting injured was the best thing that ever happened to me."

Penny didn't say anything, but he saw the questions swimming in her eyes. He also saw concern. And affection. And something else that looked a whole lot like…

No. Stay focused.

"Turned out, I needed surgery to heal the injury. The doctor said I'd be able to play football again after I recovered, but he didn't advise it."

"I imagine your dad wasn't too thrilled about that."

"Nope." The word came out on a cynical laugh. "He was dead set on getting me back on the field, no matter what the cost." His mouth twisted in distaste as he parroted his father's words. "Wanted to make sure he got a 'good return on his investment.'"

"That's just awful," Penny said.

"That's Dad," Matthew retorted.

"How did *you* feel about the diagnosis?" she persisted.

"In a weird way, relieved," he admitted. "If I walked away, the pressure would finally be off and I could figure out what I really wanted to do with my life." Matthew frowned as memories of difficult conversations began to resurface. "Of course, that wasn't the easiest thing to communicate to my father."

"I'm sure. Especially after your parents moved to be closer to you."

Matthew was surprised. "How did you know about that?" he asked, angling a sly glance her way.

Penny's eyes widened before they darted away. "I…may have asked Morgan about you on occasion."

His eyebrows rose. "Oh, really?"

"Yes, really," Penny replied, her cheeks tinged pink by something other than the frigid winter air. "But only until you graduated, which wasn't very long."

"Mmm, almost a year, by my count," Matthew joked, thoroughly enjoying getting under her skin.

"Oh, stop it," Penny chided, bumping her shoulder against his before repositioning her hands atop the railing. "That was a long time ago. Besides, you promised to behave yourself, remember? Keep that up and you'll end up on the naughty list."

Matthew laughed at the unconventional reminder. "Yours or Santa's?"

"Both."

"All right, fine," he agreed. "You're right. As usual."

Penny didn't reply, but the corners of her lips edged up on a secretive smile. "I'll try not to rub it in."

Matthew released a low chuckle. "How very considerate of you."

Penny laughed, relaxed again. "So what happened next?"

"After my injury and those terrible grades, I decided to drop out of school," Matthew said, picking up the narrative. "Of course, Dad wouldn't hear of it. For a good week, all we did was argue. I got to the end of my patience pretty quick, and when I did, I emptied my savings, bought a cheap car, packed up, and just started driving.

"But I wasn't running aimlessly. I may not have had a house in town anymore, but Cedar Ridge was always home to me, so I found my way back here."

"What did you do when you got back?"

Matthew felt his mouth twitch in response to her earnest questions. Penny was hanging on his words like he was re-telling an epic journey, not a day-long road trip in a noisy, dirty sedan.

"Didn't make it. That old car broke down a few miles outside town, which is where Mac Conlin found me, kicking at a tire."

"Mac Conlin?" Penny gave him a quizzical look. "That name doesn't ring a bell."

Matthew wasn't surprised. Besides being a natural introvert, Mac had become a bit of a recluse after his wife passed, almost fifteen years before their meeting.

"Mac was a quiet guy," Matthew relayed. "He kind of kept to himself out here."

"Oh." Penny nodded. "Okay. So this property is his?"

"Yep. All this," Matthew gestured to the cabin behind them, along with the smaller guest cabin and the workshop that stood between them. "All of it was Mac's. When he found me, he didn't say much. Just told me to follow him. He led me here." Matthew pointed to the guest cabin. "That became my home, and Mac became my mentor. He taught me everything I know about carpentry. And when..." Matthew's throat closed at the thought, but he pushed the words through. "When he died, he left his home and his business to me."

"So that's who you're mourning." Penny's voice was low, her expression soft with sympathy.

Matthew swallowed hard, knowing how keenly she understood. "Yeah."

A moment passed before Penny whispered, "When did he pass?"

"Last year, around this time."

Exactly one year tomorrow, to be precise.

"I'm so sorry," she offered. Then she apologized anew. "Sorry. I promised myself I'd never say that after my mom died. It never helps to hear."

"Maybe not, but it's something that people say when they care," Matthew suggested. "And that's what really helps."

"I guess," Penny agreed. She dropped her gaze to her hands and studied them for a long moment. "Not that I don't appreciate you sharing all that with me," she began. "But what exactly does this have to do with your murals?"

Matthew hesitated. How much should he share? His heart said everything, but fear said just enough.

"That's just it," Matthew answered. "The artwork you're trying to market isn't mine. It's Mac's."

Thin eyebrows drew close as she hummed an affirmation. "So this was never about diversifying your business."

"No," he replied. "Not at all. I'm not looking to become famous or sell a bunch of murals just for the heck of it. This is my way of honoring Mac."

A twinge of his conscience gave him pause. That wasn't entirely true.

Tell her.

Matthew heeded that still, small voice for just a moment before deciding against it. It may have been his intention to come clean, but now that the moment had come, he couldn't find it in him to disclose the real reason he was stuck on this particular project.

"Okay."

The word sounded light and optimistic. Kind of like the glow that was radiating from her eyes. Like a shaft of light in a darkened room, it bid him to drop the heavy load of guilt he was carrying and come forward into the sun. He wanted to. But something inside of him resisted.

"This changes everything."

Matthew could almost see the ideas taking shape in her mind. It lent a new warmth to his heavy heart.

"This *explains* everything," she continued, fixing her luminous eyes on him.

"I know you don't want to be on camera, but would it be all right if I record you talking about Mac?"

"Sure," he said, shrugging. "No problem."

"Excellent!" The word was punctuated by a gleeful clap of her hands. "In that case… I have an idea!"

Hope does not disappoint.

Penny stopped in her Bible reading to let the words sink in. Given her ongoing struggle between hope and fear, they seemed especially poignant today.

Morgan said this would happen when she started reading her Bible again, that the words would come to life and speak to her situation. But was Penny brave enough to believe them?

"Knock, knock." Like an answer to prayer, Morgan appeared at Penny's door, her green flannel pajamas a stark contrast to Penny's fuzzy red reindeer ones. Penny sent up a silent thank-you when she caught sight of Morgan's relaxed smile. She'd noticed a huge improvement in her friend's mood since coming home.

"Hey, you've started without me," Morgan chided, spying the open Bible in her hands. "Not that I can really fault you for it." She took a seat on the bed across from her, then peeked at Penny's Bible before opening her own, her wavy auburn hair sliding down to cover her face as she did so. "Where are you?"

"Romans 5:5."

Morgan flipped her hair back and turned to the page, humming as she read the verse. "Wow. Pretty appropriate, wouldn't you say?"

"That's what I thought, too," Penny confessed. "It's reassuring, but also a little scary."

"How so?" Morgan queried.

"I mean, I want to believe it," Penny explained. "But I've already been disappointed before, and badly. I'm not sure I'm ready to risk feeling that way again."

"Ah." Morgan nodded. "I see. Try reading the whole verse again."

"'Hope does not disappoint,'" Penny said, obliging. "'Because the love of God has been poured out into our hearts through the Holy Spirit that has been given to us.'"

"And?"

She looked up again to find Morgan eyeing her with a raised eyebrow.

"And...what?"

"Penny, what did you put your faith in before?"

"Um..." Penny had to really think about that one. While she had never outright denied the existence of God, she had stopped counting on Him in her life a long time ago. So whom had she relied on?

"Myself, I guess." The admission caused a palpable shift somewhere inside her chest. Freed from yet another unknown burden, she sat up taller.

It was true. All this time, Penny had focused on herself, her career, her way. How had she never realized before how terribly self-absorbed she'd become?

"Bingo!" Morgan beamed, her trademark megawatt smile shining brighter than ever. "And how did that make you feel?"

"Exhausted," Penny answered truthfully. "And stressed. There was always something to take care of or worry about. Everything was always on my shoulders."

"And that, I'm guessing, is probably why you were so taken

with Nick," Morgan ventured. "He seemed like someone who really cared, who could share the load."

Penny's gaze skittered away. She was embarrassed by her selfishness, not to mention her astoundingly poor judgment. "Morgan, how is it possible that you can know me better than I do?"

"Been there and done that," she remarked gently. "You're not the first person to mistake humans for God."

Penny worried her lip, deep in thought. "Is that what I've been doing?"

"Sure," Morgan replied easily. "You expected to find security, love, and fulfillment in people, when the only one who can give you those things is God. People *can* fail you. So, of course, you've been disappointed before. But when you put your faith in the one who can never disappoint, everything changes."

"How so?"

"God loves you, Penny. He cares about what's going on in your life and He wants to be a part of it." Morgan raised a finger as she quoted, "'All things work together for good to them that love God.' You'll get to that verse soon, it's in Romans."

"So you're saying that everything is working for your good?" Penny clarified. "Even Brendan cheating on you? Do you really believe that?"

"It sure didn't feel that way at first," Morgan admitted softly. "But I do now. It gave me the push I needed to take a risk by applying to the Returning Residents program. In a weird way, Brendan's actions gave me courage to pursue the fresh start I needed. And that's brought me here to you." She bumped Penny's shoulder. "Which is a good thing, too, because you need a *lot* of help."

Penny chuckled, then sobered as the reality of Morgan's words sunk in.

"God brought me you," Penny realized. "But I wouldn't have been here either if…"

Her words trailed off as her gaze collided with her friend's. Shocked as Penny was, Morgan didn't seem the least bit surprised.

"Life may seem random or even unfair sometimes, but God's always got things under control." A wink punctuated her next remark. "Things do tend to go a lot more smoothly when you work with Him, though."

Penny smiled alongside her. "Noted."

"The point is," Morgan continued, "whenever I trust in God, I'm never disappointed. I see His hand in everything, and He always takes care of me."

"I've almost forgotten what it's like to have someone take care of me." The somber statement came out on a weary breath. Penny was more than ready for that to change.

Morgan's lips slanted into a sly grin in response. "I think I know a certain contractor who might beg to differ."

Penny rolled her eyes, unable to suppress a smile at the turn this conversation was taking. "Really, Morgan?"

"Really, Penny," she insisted. "Or are you going to try and convince me that you're sitting in here worrying about something *other* than how Matthew might respond to your situation?"

Once again, Penny's mouth fell open in response to her friend's perception.

"Come on, Penny," she teased. "You and I both know your poker face could use some serious work."

Penny had to laugh. "All right, fine, you caught me. I'm worried about Matthew. Now what?"

"Now, you trust that He'll work everything out for your good," Morgan said. "Let Him lead you, Penny. You'll know in your heart what to do."

Penny ran an absentminded hand over the embroidered

comforter beneath her as she considered Morgan's words. Her best friend comes home after the worst betrayal of her life, and yet, here she is mere days later, confidently expounding on the goodness of God. How had her faith not been shaken? How could she still be so joyful?

Penny wanted what Morgan had. She knew it in an instant, in a moment of insight that left no doubt in her mind. She didn't just want a relationship with God. She *needed* it.

"I think I'm ready."

A light hand on her shoulder reassured her. "I know you are."

Penny nodded, the action slight yet resolute. "Let's pray."

"That's my girl!" Morgan's encouraging smile solidified Penny's resolve. "While we're at it, I've got a situation to offer up as well."

"Sure. What's up?"

"Do you remember my friend Anne Carlyle?"

Penny blinked. "The woman who runs the shelter for single moms?"

"That's the one." Morgan nodded. "I just heard from her a few days ago. Turns out the building they're renting just got sold to a developer, so now they're looking for a new home."

Though Penny's acquaintance with Saving Grace was limited to what Morgan had shared about her time volunteering there, her stories had made a lasting impression. Anne did more than simply refer the women in her care to other services or hand out resources. She personally took them in, taught them necessary life skills, and secured stable jobs and affordable housing for them. Saving Grace seemed more like a family than a shelter. And now, it was in danger of closing?

"That's terrible," Penny sympathized.

"Yeah, it is," Morgan responded. "But God will provide. In the meantime, let's lift them up in prayer."

"Of course," Penny quickly agreed. "I just wish there was something more that we could do."

"It might not feel like it, but praying is the best thing we can do." Morgan shrugged. "Although I know what you mean. Sometimes you just want to dive in and tackle a problem instead of praying for guidance first. I've definitely been guilty of that."

"You? Really?"

Morgan angled her a sly glance in response to her teasing. "Watch it."

Penny laughed before boldly declaring, "I'm choosing to hope. Anything's possible, right?"

"Absolutely."

Chapter Nine

"No peeking!" Walking backward with one hand on either arm, Cassandra gleefully guided Morgan through the threshold as they entered her salon for the big reveal.

"Oh, my," Penny breathed, taking it all in. "This place is incredible!"

Cassandra clasped her hands together in eager anticipation. "You like it?"

"I *love* it." Penny beamed.

"And I'd love for you to stop talking about it so that I can finally see it!" Morgan joked.

"Okay, sorry!" Cassandra shot a decidedly unapologetic wink in Penny's direction. "Are you ready?"

"So ready," Morgan replied. Beside her, Penny smiled wide. She knew how much this fresh start meant to Morgan, and she couldn't be happier for her.

"Okay, on three," Cassandra said. "One, two…three!"

Morgan opened her eyes and gasped. True to Cassandra's word, teal was the star—gracing the trim work and sinks and contrasting the creamy whites and natural woods beautifully. Morgan would feel right at home in the beachy, relaxed space.

Penny turned and found her trembling as tears streamed silently down her face.

"Morgan?" she ventured.

Her friend nodded silently, one hand over her heart and the other at her lips. "It's perfect," she breathed, blinking fast.

Penny wrapped an arm around her shoulder and Cassandra soon joined in.

"Thank you so much," Morgan said to the budding designer on a tight squeeze. "I can't believe this is my space."

"You're so welcome," Cassandra replied. "Thank *you* for trusting me."

With shaky hands, Morgan carefully swiped underneath her eyes as the girls parted.

"Come on," Cassandra prompted.

"Let's take a closer look at your space."

As she led Morgan away, bells tinkled overhead. Turning quickly, Penny felt a twinge of disappointment when she found Gwen standing in the entryway.

"Sorry I'm late," she apologized, taking a moment to smooth out her wind-blown hair. "An out-of-towner arrived for the grand opening, and I didn't want to turn her away."

"Really? We've got visitors already?" Penny asked. "The grand opening is still a week away."

"Yeah, I think she said she's a reporter from Ann Arbor. Apparently, Mayor Bennett called her in to do a report on the Returning Residents program."

"Ah, okay." Penny's excitement settled somewhat. It seemed that crowds of tourists weren't descending upon their little town just yet. And though it was wonderful to hear that Cedar Ridge would soon be spotlighted in a large Michigan publication, only time would tell if their plan would turn out to be a success in the long term.

"Morgan, you remember my friend, Gwen, right?" Cassandra asked, making introductions.

"Of course," Morgan replied, stepping forward to give Gwen a hug. "It's great to see you."

"You too," Gwen returned the gesture. "So what do you

think?" she asked as she pulled away, nodding in Cassandra's direction. "Did she pass?"

"With flying colors." Morgan beamed. "And I do mean that literally."

Gwen chuckled. "Even the sinks?"

"Yes, I *love* them," Morgan said, gushing.

"Right?" Cassandra chimed in. "Can you believe I got them for almost a quarter of the original price?"

"Um, *yes*," Gwen scoffed playfully. "Who else would want teal sinks?"

As the girls caught up, Penny took the opportunity to sneak a peek at her phone. There was no message from Matthew. He hadn't said as much, but Penny had assumed he would be here today, especially given how much work he'd put into the salon. Where else could he be?

"Matt isn't coming."

Cassandra's voice broke into her thoughts and made her jump.

"Sorry," she quickly apologized.

"It's fine," Penny reassured her.

Just another jolt to her already weary heart. No big deal.

"Today is a rough day for Matt, so I wouldn't be surprised if he's MIA. But if I had to guess, I'd say he'd probably be at the cemetery right about now."

Understanding finally dawned. "Is today when…?"

"Yep." Cassandra's nod confirmed her suspicions. "Last year, today."

"I wonder why he didn't say anything," Penny said, pondering aloud.

"In case you haven't noticed, he's not a real chatty guy," Cassandra replied, her smile sympathetic and soft. "At least, not when it comes to Mac. But just the same, I think he'd appreciate a visit from you."

"You think?"

"No," Cassandra amended. "I *know*."

* * *

Matthew wasn't sure how long he'd been sitting on the wrought-iron bench, but the pileup of snow on the sleeves of his jacket was telling.

He blew out a sigh, then watched his breath float away on a crystallized puff.

"I'm sorry, Mac."

The words slipped out unexpectedly. Not that that surprised him anymore. It happened often enough. Now, if only those apologies would start to make a difference. No matter how many times he uttered those words, it never seemed like enough. Sorry wouldn't bring his mentor back. Sorry was just wishful thinking.

Another sigh.

"This is all my fault." He scrubbed a hand across his face. "It should have been me."

Those words made the weight of guilt sitting on his chest feel even heavier than usual, but that was the truth. Mac was gone, and Matthew had no one to blame but himself.

The sound of crunching snow startled him, and he turned to see who it was.

Penny.

A cold wave of dread washed over him. When had she gotten here? And what exactly had she heard?

The cautious expression on her face gave nothing away. Nothing but discomfort, that is. Matthew had seen that look a hundred times before, on as many faces. It seemed she didn't know how to proceed, or what would be best. But still, she was here.

"Hi."

Her tentative tone matched the uncertain expression to a tee. As morose as he felt, she never failed to lift his spirits.

"Hey," he returned, more easily than expected. "What are you doing out here?"

She shifted her weight between her feet. "A little birdie might have told me that today is...*the* day."

Matthew had a feeling he knew exactly who that little birdie was. His meddling older sister, of course. "Yeah," he said. "It is."

"Why didn't you tell me?"

Matthew's heart squeezed tightly in response to the hurt in her voice.

"Didn't seem important." He shrugged.

"Of course, it is," she insisted. "If it's important to you..." The words trailed off as she took a small step forward, almost as if she'd been taken aback by the earnestness of her response. Instantly, her trademark shyness returned full force.

"I thought that it might help if you had some company." She stepped away, almost as if trying to undo her earlier action. "But if not, that's fine, too. I can leave if you want."

Matthew nodded toward the opposite end of the bench. "Come sit down."

Penny obliged, perching on the edge of the bench and folding her hands in her lap. At first, she squinted at the tombstone, reading the words etched onto its surface. Then she surreptitiously stole a glance in his direction, her cheeks taking on a pretty shade of pink when she caught him watching her.

"Sorry," she said, faltering.

He fought a small twitch at the corner of his lips. "For what?"

"I don't know," she replied on a nervous laugh. "I guess I'm just not sure of how to act in these kinds of situations. Ironic, isn't it?"

"Just be you," he replied.

She nodded, a sweet smile on her face. "Okay." Then her eyes flicked up to a spot above his gaze. "You, um, you have some snow... Actually, a lot of snow."

She gestured toward his hair and Matthew ran a hand through it. "Better?"

Her lopsided smile was telling. "Kind of."

She slid closer and gently brushed away the rest of the snow, first from his hair and then from his shoulders. Her fingers barely touched him, but her affection reached deep into his heart.

His gaze stayed riveted on her face, reveling in her every movement as she tenderly swept away the offending powder. Once finished, her eyes met his and he heard her draw in a tremulous breath. Instinctively, Matthew reached for those delicate fingers and enfolded them between his hands.

"You've been out here for a while." It was a statement, not a question, punctuated by the soft glow of concern that illuminated her eyes.

"Yeah." His voice sounded raspy to his ears. He cleared his throat. "Are my hands too cold?"

"No." She dropped her gaze to their intertwined fingers. "Not at all. I just wish I'd thought to bring you something warm to drink."

"It's fine," he replied. "Just you being here is enough."

Penny smiled, but it was frayed.

"What?" he asked, immediately suspicious.

"Nothing," she quickly replied.

"Come on, what is it?"

Her worried eyes darted to the ground. "I wasn't trying to eavesdrop," she began.

"Ah." Matthew knew where this was going. "You overheard me."

"What do you mean it should have been you?" Her eyes were on him again, wide and sad and soulful. "Do you really think you should have…died?"

Her voice cracked on the word, rending his heart in the process.

Matthew drew in a deep breath of crisp winter air. There was no more hiding from the truth. This time, he had to come clean and share the entire story.

"Penny, the night Mac died, he was making a delivery," Matthew explained. "*My* delivery. I was supposed to drive a custom dresser over to Ann Arbor, but I had been working on a different project that morning and lost track of time. When he realized I hadn't left, Mac came out to the workshop to remind me. Then when he saw me up to my ears in sawdust, he volunteered to go instead. Said he didn't want to interrupt my 'flow.' He made the delivery, but..." Matthew's throat closed at the thought. He cleared it and forced himself to continue. "His truck slid on a patch of black ice on the way home. He never made it."

"Oh, Matthew," Penny sympathized. "I don't know what to say."

Matthew shrugged. There wasn't much anyone could say. Mac was gone, and it was all his fault. Period, end of story.

"If I had gone instead," he continued, "if I'd insisted, if I hadn't been so careless..." He turned to face the plot in the ground that housed his friend and mentor. "I don't know. But I just feel like I should have done it differently. And because I didn't, he's gone. I'm the reason he died."

A long moment passed before she spoke.

"That isn't fair." Penny's voice was stronger now, her conviction plain. "Matthew, you can't keep carrying this all by yourself. Mac's death was an accident. It's not your fault."

It sure *felt* like he was the one responsible.

"Do you believe me?"

When he didn't answer, Penny wiggled one hand free from his grasp and used it to cup his cheek.

"Matthew." His breath caught when he glimpsed the compassion in her eyes. "Do you believe me?"

"I can't."

"Why not?"

When he didn't offer an answer, Penny changed tactics.

"What if the roles were reversed?" she asked. "What if Mac had been the one to miss a delivery? What would you have done?"

"I would have jumped in to help him," Matthew admitted.

"If you had gotten hurt along the way, would you have blamed him?"

"No. Of course not."

Even if his conscience hadn't been pricked by that response, Penny's knowing look would have driven her point home, regardless.

"If I posed that same question to Mac, do you think he'd answer differently?"

"No." Matthew saw where she was going but wasn't certain he was ready to follow.

"So if he wouldn't blame you, why are you putting the blame on yourself?"

"It's not that simple, Penny," he whispered. "Mac took me in. Changed my life. He didn't owe me anything. I'm the one who owes him."

Penny's expression changed at that admission. "Owe him?" she repeated, incredulous. Her hand drew back, leaving a cold spot on his cheek where it once rested. "I'm sorry, but love doesn't work that way."

He frowned. "What do you mean?"

"Mac took you in because he wanted to. He taught you for the same reason. Not because he had to, or because he expected anything in return. Right?"

"Yeah."

"Clearly, Mac loved you," Penny concluded. "And love doesn't count the cost. It just gives."

He had to admit, she had a point. Matthew would have to think long and hard about that. In the meantime, he preoccupied himself by tucking a few stray wisps of hair behind her ear.

"Don't try to distract me," she warned, fighting against a smirk and losing.

Matthew chuckled. "Pretty sure you're the one distracting me."

Penny narrowed her eyes. "Boy, do you play dirty."

A laugh escaped from his lips before he could think the better of it. Almost instantly, he tensed, as if trying to contain his rebellious breath.

This was no time for laughter.

"Matthew, I know you had it rough with your own father," Penny whispered. "I know the kind of love he offered you was conditional. But Mac is not your dad, and neither is God. Both of them love you for who you are, not what you do. Both have forgiven you. Now, you need to forgive yourself."

Her words stirred hope to life inside his heart. Everything Penny was saying was true. The peace her words brought to his soul was testimony of that. They sounded good. But more than that, they felt *right*. Why hadn't he been able to see things differently until now?

"Is that what you've done?"

Her eyes widened in shock. "What *I've* done? What do you mean?"

"With Andrew," Matthew clarified. "Have you forgiven yourself for leaving town without him?"

"I haven't thought about it like that before," Penny confessed. "But you're right, my words apply to me, too. Andrew doesn't seem mad at me, so why am I being so hard on myself? It's probably time I stop beating myself up about the decisions I made as a kid."

"Probably?" he asked, pleased when he saw a little smile emerge in response to his teasing.

"Definitely," she amended.

"Good." He reached an arm around her shoulders and tucked her close. "So we have a deal? I'll forgive myself if you forgive yourself?"

A muffled chuckle sounded somewhere close to his heart. "We're not even through our first deal and now you want to strike a new one?"

"What can I say?" he replied easily. "We make a great team."

Penny wrapped an arm around his waist and huddled closer. "You're right about that."

Matthew's heart swelled until it felt fit to burst.

He barely managed to hold back a laugh. The fact that he even felt good enough to laugh today surprised him. It almost seemed wrong to be happy on the anniversary of Mac's death. But Penny was spot on with her assessment. Punishing himself wasn't going to bring his mentor back any more than his unceasing apologies would. It was time to make peace with the past and move forward.

With Penny.

All at once, Matthew knew that Cassandra and Gwen were right. For as long as he kept his true feelings for Penny a secret, Matthew risked losing her for good. If he stood a chance of convincing her to stay in Cedar Ridge permanently, he had to take the initiative and tell her how he felt.

"Penny?" he breathed.

She leaned back just enough so she could look him in the eye. "Yes?"

"Thank you for coming to find me," he whispered. "It means a lot to have you here."

And soon, she would know just how much. But Matthew had to find the right way to tell her first. Something special. Something worthy of her.

"Of course." A quiet peace settled in her expression, complementing the warmth in her blue-gray depths and the relaxed smile that graced her perfect lips. Returning her head to his shoulder, she waited a beat, then asked, "Tell me about Mac."

Then, with more peace than he ever thought possible, Matthew obliged.

Penny stood by the window the following day, anticipation thrumming through her veins. Her every nerve was on alert, but it was a pleasant excitement that she wouldn't trade for the world.

Underneath that excitement, however, was uncertainty. In the moment, she had relished spending time with Matthew and feeling so close to him. But once home, the truth of their situation sunk in with vivid clarity.

Matthew had experienced a loss that had shaken him to his core. If Penny truly cared about him, shouldn't she be trying to protect him from a repeat of that grief?

But that wasn't what she was doing at all. On the contrary, she had grown lax over the past few weeks, putting aside the reality of her heart condition to revel in the closeness and connection she felt with Matthew.

Maybe hope had gotten the better of her. Or maybe it was all the optimism that came along with the Christmas season. Either way, she wanted to believe in a happy ending. To trust that Mathew might be different, and that he would respond to her situation with empathy, not rejection.

But Penny had only been considering her side of the story, without a thought to how hard another loss might be on Matthew.

As long as there was a threat to her health, wouldn't the kindest course of action be to keep her distance, at least until after her surgery? Then maybe, if she felt better, if her condition stabilized…

Penny released a tired breath. There were those "ifs" again, trying their best to unsettle her. Even just one short week ago,

Penny might have succumbed to their taunts and thrown herself a one-woman pity party. Today, she opted to fight against the heaviness pulling at her heart by surrendering the situation to God, like Morgan had taught her.

Lord, I don't know what's going to happen to me, or how Matthew will feel about it, but I trust that You have a plan, and that You will take care of us.

In the meantime, she would keep her distance. It may not be what she wanted, but it was the right thing to do.

Too bad she had impulsively invited Matthew to attend their Christmas tree decorating party, which was due to start any minute. Unfortunately for Penny, avoiding the attractive contractor would be much more easily said than done.

"Looking for your date?"

The words, spoken right beside her ear, made Penny jump. "Morgan!"

"What?" Her friend simply laughed, her green eyes bright. "Don't blame me if your daydreams are louder than my footsteps."

Penny rolled her eyes, but couldn't prevent a smile from spreading across her face. "You're too much, you know that?"

"I'm choosing to take that as a compliment," Morgan replied. "But seriously, is he on his way?"

"Should be."

"Ooh, I am so proud of you," Morgan cooed, throwing in a gentle bump of Penny's shoulder for good measure. "Way to make the first move."

Under normal circumstances, her obvious teasing would have made Penny laugh, but she was far too busy fending off her embarrassment to take part in her best friend's fun today.

"What first move?" she protested, already feeling the heat of embarrassment start to rise. "This isn't a date, it's a Christmas-tree-decorating party."

Besides, she thought, snuggling with Matthew out in the

cold more than qualified as a romantic advance, didn't it? The first move was already spoken for. The second would have to wait.

She didn't realize she'd lost herself in thought again until Morgan's expression changed.

"Wait a minute." Narrowed eyes bored into Penny as a Cheshire-cat smile erupted across Morgan's face. "Something happened yesterday, didn't it?"

"Morgan!" Penny admonished. "Don't be ridiculous."

"Oh, I'm right!" she exclaimed, paying no heed to Penny's warning. "Did he kiss you?"

"What? No!"

"Did he try to?"

"No! Morgan, please," Penny begged, sneaking a peek around her friend's back to make sure that Andrew and Nana were still tucked away in the kitchen, safely out of earshot. "I'll tell you later, once everyone's gone."

"Okay, fine," Morgan relented. "I'll cut you some slack. How about you come to my place after the party? No one will overhear you there."

"That sounds perfect," Penny agreed.

That would also give her some more time to sort out her racing thoughts before trying to explain them to Morgan.

"Great." Morgan's sly smile warned Penny that a good-natured jab was on its way. "But just a heads-up, your cheeks are redder than a holly berry right now."

Penny's hands flew up to her face. "Oh, dear."

Morgan released a gentle laugh. "I know, I've been a terrible friend, getting under your skin right before your second date."

"Like I said, this is not a date."

"Ri-i-i-ght," Morgan agreed, but the exaggerated wink she sent Penny's way strongly begged to differ. "I'd better let you cool off before your boyfriend gets here."

Penny perched a hand on her hip in response. "I can't wait

until it's your turn to fall in love. I'm not going to let you hear the end of it."

Morgan's entire countenance lit up at her choice of words. "Love?"

"I didn't mean it like that," Penny said, backpedaling with hands raised in surrender.

Only, that didn't feel right to say. On the contrary, a pinprick of her conscience told her that her verbal slip was anything but accidental.

Was she really falling in love with Matthew?

Not that it would be so difficult to do. Caring about Matthew felt as effortless as breathing, and about as essential. But her heart…

"Right." Morgan's shift into maternal mode told Penny that her perceptive friend understood her unspoken dilemma. "So you're in deep, huh?"

Penny drew in a long breath, then exhaled. "Maybe."

Morgan hummed an affirmation as she nodded, sympathy momentarily stirring in her eyes before turning to melancholy. "It's not such a bad thing, you know. Falling in love. It's a gift from God, so you might as well enjoy it."

Penny felt like the biggest heel. Here she was talking about falling for Matthew, while Morgan was still mourning the hopes she'd had for her own broken relationship. "Morgan, I'm so sorry. I shouldn't have—"

A hand raised to stop her flow of words.

"Don't. Yes, I've been through a lot, but that doesn't mean I can't be happy for you." Her words were even, quiet, calm… and thoroughly unconvincing. "You're right," Morgan continued, nodding her head slowly. "My time will come. One day."

Penny didn't know what to say. Instead of risking a bigger blunder, she chose to keep her big mouth shut.

"But that doesn't change the fact that your time is happening right now."

"That isn't true."

Morgan sent a raised eyebrow her way. "I think it is."

"But, Morgan, what about my heart condition? Matthew's already lost someone close to him, and that was only a year ago." She swallowed hard, doing her best to keep the memories of Nick's abrupt about-face at bay. "What if he doesn't want to go through all that again?"

"Penny, I know you're scared," Morgan began, resting a caring hand on her shoulder to ground Penny's flyaway worries. "And you can entertain the what ifs for as long as you'd like. But wondering will only get you so far. There's really only one way to find out how Matthew feels about your condition, and that's by telling him."

Penny shook her head, unconvinced. "Besides, isn't staying away from him to protect him from loss the most caring thing that I can do?"

Morgan tilted her head to consider her better. Penny responded by turning away to resume her post looking out the window.

"Are you sure you're not just running away again?"

"What do you mean?"

"I think we both know that your approach to fear is typically to run and hide," Morgan explained. She pointed a finger at the distance between them. "Or are you going to come up with another reason for backing away from me?"

Penny felt her shoulders slump. Morgan had her, there.

"I know it's tempting to justify that fear with virtue, but disguising that tendency isn't going to help you overcome it. Ignoring the problem isn't going to make it go away. You've got to face this, Penny."

"I know," Penny replied, her voice low. "But that's a lot easier said than done."

She heard Morgan step closer, then felt two hands give her shoulders a little squeeze.

"Have a little faith," Morgan encouraged her. "I have a feeling that Matthew will surprise you."

That, thought Penny somberly, was exactly what she was afraid of.

"What in the world is this supposed to be?"

Standing before a large cardboard box, Matthew held up the ornament in question—a macaroni collage that had seen better days.

"That, good sir, is the world's most innovative interpretation of a reindeer." Andrew's retort came from somewhere behind the Christmas tree, where he was working on stringing the lights. "Immortalized by dried noodles and craft glue."

Beside Penny, Morgan snorted. "Looks more like a Christmas liberty bell."

"A Christmas liberty bell sure beats that stack of doilies you tried to pass off as a snowflake."

Morgan gave a mock gasp. "How dare you? I worked really hard on that!"

Penny stole a glance at Matthew amid their friendly bickering. Based on the secretive grin he seemed to be wrestling with, he was just as amused as she was.

Morgan's words were still ringing in her ears, but she wasn't ready to come clean about her heart condition just yet.

It wasn't the right time, she reasoned. At a Christmas party, among her family and friend? No, her confession could wait a little while longer.

While she and Matthew unearthed more ornaments and her brother and best friend exchanged words, Nana set a tray of finger sandwiches on the coffee table, then tapped Penny's shoulder. "There are a few more snacks in the kitchen, dear. Would you mind getting the rest for me?"

"Of course, Nana," Penny agreed.

"Thank you, sweetie."

Nana only waited until Penny turned to leave before asking Matthew to accompany her granddaughter. Penny could have rolled her eyes at the obvious matchmaking attempt, but out of respect for her grandmother, she refrained. Andrew and Morgan, however, did no such thing.

"Are you sure you want to send those two alone, Nana?" Andrew jeered, their bickering temporarily forgotten.

"Only if she hung some mistletoe up first." Morgan winked.

Penny groaned. "That's enough, you two."

She passed through the doorway without a second glance, Matthew close behind her.

"I like the way she thinks," he commented.

So did Penny, but she had to be more careful, for both their sakes.

"I already checked the house for booby traps," she joked. "All clear."

"That's too bad."

Her breath caught and held. If only she could act on her feelings for Matthew instead of pushing them away. But with her heart literally hanging in the balance, Penny had no choice but to keep her distance. Even though that was the absolute last thing she wanted to do.

Stepping into the kitchen, Penny caught sight of a plate piled high with assorted Christmas cookies, and another with bite-size sandwiches held together with colorful toothpicks. Warm cider simmered gently in a saucepan on the stove, and a pitcher of punch sat on the counter next to an impressive trifle.

Penny bit back an unexpected surge of emotion. This scene looked very familiar.

"Wow, she really went all out," Matthew innocently commented.

"Yeah."

The brief affirmative was all Penny could manage as memories of the Christmas parties once hosted by her mother played in her mind's eye. She clenched her jaw against the recollections, then willfully relaxed.

It was getting easier to allow herself to feel these days. A few weeks ago, Penny would have tried to ignore the ache in her chest, to numb the pain instead of giving it permission to pass through her. But now, she was finding that the joy housed in her memories far outlasted the momentary discomfort they might initially induce. And the more she relaxed and remembered, the happier she became.

Now, if only her conflicted feelings for Matthew would resolve themselves, too.

"I'll get the punch," Penny announced a little too brightly, moving to grab the pitcher.

The sooner they returned to the living room, the sooner she would be out of the danger zone.

It wasn't that she didn't want to spend time with him. She did. Penny just wasn't sure of what to do with all the feelings he stirred to life. All she wanted was to rejoice in their new beginning. But how could she when her heart put her very life in jeopardy?

"I've got it." Matthew moved to take the pitcher from her hands, but in her hurry, Penny all but collided with him, sending punch sloshing in every direction.

"Sorry," he said, cringing. "It looked heavy."

"No," she quickly amended, avoiding his gaze. "It was my fault."

She tried to turn away, but large hands caught her elbows and held on. "Hey."

She froze at his touch, her gaze moving up to find his eyebrows drawn and his handsome mouth in a slight frown as he studied her.

How could he be so devastatingly handsome even while frowning? It just wasn't fair.

Penny held back a frustrated huff. Nothing about this situation was fair. But there was no use in letting herself get so flustered when it wasn't going to change the situation.

"Did I do something to upset you?"

Matthew's gentle words broke through her vexation like a ray of sunlight through a storm cloud.

"No." Penny nearly sighed as the word escaped on a suddenly weary breath. "You didn't."

Seemingly reassured that she wouldn't try to run away again, Matthew slid his hands down her arms, then gently pried the pitcher out of her hands. He set it down on the counter before turning back toward her.

Penny opened her mouth to speak, but the words died in her throat when he slipped an arm around her waist and drew her close. Instinctively, her hands came to rest on his broad chest, her heart thundering louder than any storm.

"So what's going on?" he whispered. "Talk to me."

Penny tried frantically to think of a good reason to be avoiding him, but the feel of warm fingers brushing away loose strands of hair was making that nearly impossible.

"It's nothing to do with you," Penny said, almost pleading, willing him to understand. "I promise."

Concern still mingled with the affection shining in his soft emerald eyes. The combination found her leaning closer, her heart practically pushing her toward him. Surprise registered briefly in his gaze before turning into contentment. He leaned forward, too. Anticipation thrummed through her veins, but once it reached her heart, it grabbed hold and squeezed tight.

Penny tried to keep from crying out as an unexpected pain cut across her chest, but a quick breath escaped her lips despite her best efforts. Matthew's gaze flicked back up to hers, his expression faraway, as if he was struggling to wake up from a dream.

Keep it together, she coached herself. *Don't let him see...*

"I think I get it," he finally concluded.

Penny's heart stopped and took a free fall to her toes. "You do?"

"Yeah. All that teasing can wear on anybody, much less a natural introvert like you."

The tidal wave of relief that washed over her was so strong, Penny's knees threatened to give out from under her. Or was that just another symptom?

"You probably felt all kinds of uncomfortable back there," he went on. "With Andrew and Morgan drawing so much attention to us."

"Yeah," she agreed. "That's accurate."

Just not for the reason he was thinking. Sharp pains were now clawing at her chest, making this conversation anything but comfortable.

For what felt like the millionth time, Penny questioned whether it was worth keeping her secret if the stress of carrying it was aggravating the very condition she was trying to hide. At a loss, she sent up a silent prayer.

What should I do here, Lord? I need Your help. I don't know which way is best. Show me, please.

"But we're alone now."

Matthew's quiet observation reverberated through her mind, chasing out all competing thoughts. Dizziness threatened as her heart kicked into overdrive, every beat slamming against her chest with renewed intensity.

His hands tightened on her waist. A lazy smile played on his face. And a small voice whispered inside her heart.

Tell him.

"Looks like we didn't need that mistletoe after all."

She just about melted in response. But she couldn't let him kiss her. Not without him knowing the truth.

"Matthew," she whispered. "There's something that I—"

"What's taking so long in there?"

Penny practically leaped out of his arms at the sound of

Morgan's voice, just in time for her friend to saunter into the kitchen and stop short at the scene before her.

"What happened?"

"Just a little spill," Penny replied brightly, pushing past the piercing pain radiating from her heart to reach for the paper towels.

"I see," Morgan said, but her pensive tone told Penny that what she saw ran deep.

"It was all my fault," Matthew insisted. "I can clean it up."

Penny couldn't bring herself to look at him. Her cheeks were ablaze, along with the rest of her body, and her hands trembled as she furiously wiped down the counter.

"That's all right." Morgan stepped in. "We've got this. Don't we, Penny?"

"Sure."

Penny held back a sigh of relief. She desperately needed some space, not just to process what had almost happened, but to drop the facade and give her poor, tired heart a break. It was taking all her strength just to remain standing, and her cleaning act wasn't helping.

"Just bring the drinks to the living room," Morgan instructed, taking charge. "We'll come back with the snacks in a few minutes."

Matthew didn't say anything, but he also didn't move right away. Penny still refused to meet his gaze, for fear that he would see more than he should. When she didn't object, he did as requested and left with the cider in one hand and the punch in the other.

The moment he was out of earshot, Morgan's hand gripped her arm tight. "What happened?"

Penny stopped, leaning against the counter for support. A spot of punch stared back at her, this one underneath the juicer.

"Penny?" Morgan's voice was worried now. Penny was

worried, too. Morgan was standing right beside her, but she sounded so far away. "Are you okay?"

Penny shook her head, a pitiful gesture that didn't do her chilling uncertainty justice.

That spot of punch just didn't look right. How had the drink managed to land here, so far away from the spill?

"Penny, what is it?" A cold hand pressed against her forehead. "You don't look good."

She dragged a shaky finger through the liquid and brought it to her mouth.

Ginger?

"Penny!" Morgan grabbed her by the shoulders and pushed her toward a dining chair. "Sit! Talk!"

Penny dragged her gaze up to Morgan, but the room seemed to spin behind her. "Don't…tell anyone."

Her breath was too shallow to finish the sentence.

"Okay, I won't," Morgan quickly agreed. "But I'm calling Dr. Brooks. In the meantime, put your head down and take deep breaths."

Penny did as she was told as Morgan pulled her phone from her back pocket and dialed the number. After a brief conversation, she walked back to the group, platters in hand, and breezily announced that a delivery had shown up at the salon unexpectedly, and they would be back soon.

"Put this on." Morgan was back and draping Penny's jacket over her shoulders. "And lean on me. We're going out the back."

Clumsily, Penny obliged, marveling at how exhausted she had become and terrified of what that might mean.

"We're going to get through this," Morgan encouraged beside her. "One step at a time."

If only she could be so certain.

Chapter Ten

"What do you mean, tonight?"

Penny couldn't believe what she was hearing. Dr. Brooks couldn't possibly be serious! She and Andrew were due in Ann Arbor for the cookie contest today—she couldn't just up and leave.

"This is serious, Miss Shay," the doctor said, his gravelly voice somber through her phone's speaker. "I've called in a favor, and you're expected at the hospital tonight at five o'clock sharp."

Penny leaned back against the car seat and pinched the bridge of her nose. This could not be happening.

By the time the girls had reached Dr. Brooks's office two days ago, Penny's heart rate had slowed. After a thorough examination, he gave her something to stabilize her heart. Before long, the pain had stopped, the dizziness passed, and they were able to return to the Christmas party as if nothing had happened. Penny had thought she was in the clear.

But now she was supposed to drop everything for emergency surgery? On the same day as the cookie contest?

"But I'm needed here," she protested weakly. "Couldn't it wait just one more—"

"No, it can't." Dr. Brooks' voice was soft yet serious. "You are in real danger here, Miss Shay. It's not as if you have a choice."

Penny sighed, dropping her hand onto her lap. He was right. Her health was far more important than a cookie competition. But how was she supposed to break the news to Andrew?

She agreed, thanked the doctor, then hung up. For a few minutes, she waited in her car, putting off the inevitable for as long as she could before making the short walk to the bakery. Then after a quick prayer, she took the plunge.

"About time you showed up," Andrew called from the back as she walked in. "Grab an apron, we've got just enough time to take one last shot at this recipe before we have to leave."

"Andrew, can we talk?"

"We can talk on the way," he answered without so much as a glance her way. "Right now, we've got some serious baking to do."

"It's important."

Her brother paused just long enough to shoot her a perplexed frown. "Okay…"

Penny wrung her hands together, not sure of how to start.

"Well, I have some good news and some bad news. Which would you like first?"

His frown deepened as he pulled a mixing bowl from the shelf and set it onto the worktable. "The competition is tonight. We can't afford any bad news."

"I—I know," Penny spluttered. "But it's not something I can help."

Andrew leaned back against the worktable. "What's going on, Pinkie?"

Penny took a deep breath. "I…left some unfinished business in New York."

Her brother's eyebrows shot up. "Unfinished business?"

"Yes, and I have to take care of it."

Penny felt as if she was shrinking under his gaze. Old habits died hard. Pushing herself past her natural reserve, she forced herself to keep a straight posture and maintain eye contact. But it wasn't easy.

"When?" he asked simply.

She swallowed hard. She hated to disappoint Andrew, but what choice did she have?

"Tonight."

His face fell. "What? Are you kidding me?"

"Andrew, I'm sorry," she pleaded. "I can't get out of it."

"Why not?" he returned. "Why can't this wait until tomorrow? Or after Christmas?"

"It's...time-sensitive."

"Time-sensitive," he repeated, cynicism practically dripping from his words as anger clouded his face, marring his normally handsome features. "Right. I get it now."

"No, you don't."

"Oh, I think I do," he continued. "You're afraid to compete. So now, you're bailing on me. Again."

Penny sank under the familiar weight of guilt. But this time, she pushed back. "That's not fair."

"No, you know what's not fair?" His voice was calm, but the fire that flashed in those icy blue eyes took her by surprise. "The fact that I can't count on you. And I know that, but I just wanted—" He shook his head and crossed his arms. "Oh, what's the point? I can't believe I actually thought you'd changed."

Penny recoiled, his every word a heavy blow to her already wounded heart. "Andrew, I'm not leaving for years this time," she insisted. "I'll be back soon. I promise."

"Don't bother."

Penny froze, paralyzed by disbelief. He'd spoken softly. Maybe she'd misunderstood.

"You don't mean that."

"I do." He didn't look at her, but his jaw was set, his expression grim. "I need a partner that I can trust. You've proven that isn't you."

Penny drew in a shaky breath, tears threatening. "Fine." She turned to walk away, pausing at the door. Andrew hadn't moved, hadn't said anything to stop her. But he also hadn't resumed his baking.

"Just so you know, I found out the secret ingredient. Fresh ginger juice." She was met with silence, but it was answer enough for her. Swallowing past the lump that rose in her throat, Penny pronounced her next words on a wobbly breath. "Goodbye, Andy."

Then she walked through the door, got into her car, and cried.

It was a wonder Penny made it to Matthew's workshop in one piece. The tears that began in the aftermath of Andrew's reaction had yet to stop, still silently streaming down her cheeks as she drove.

To say that her heart felt shattered would be an understatement. Ripped out, stomped on, and then run over by a snowplow would be more like it. She had been right. Underneath his joking and laid-back facade, Andrew hadn't forgiven her for leaving. And why should he? It wasn't as if she'd given him any reason to. It had taken a life-threatening diagnosis to bring her back home. Why hadn't she returned sooner, for him?

Because she was a coward, that's why. Because she'd been afraid to own up to her mistakes. Because it had been easier to pretend.

That's what they had been doing, right? Pretending. But beneath the pleasantries, Andrew was still hurt. Still mad. Still the little brother she had left behind.

Penny barely saw the scenic tree-lined road, or the thin layer of pristine white snow that embellished the intricately entangled branches overhead. The awe-inspiring sight usually gave her pause. Today, it just looked barren. Lonely. Dead.

Misery slowly morphed into fear as she approached her next destination. Andrew hadn't understood. What if Matthew didn't, either? What if he told her not to come back, too?

A mournful sob caught in her throat at the thought.

Dear God, please not that.

Her fragile little heart just couldn't take it.

Penny's head throbbed as she entered the clearing that housed his workshop. Situated between a pair of cozy craftsman-style homes, complete with smoke curling up in wisps from their twin chimneys, the scene looked like something out of a Norman Rockwell painting.

Or her worst nightmare.

Drawing in slow and steady breaths, Penny tried to calm her racing heart, but the fear was uncontrollable. She sighed, completely drained of strength and questioning why she hadn't called Morgan to accompany her today.

Because you wanted to stand on your own. Because you wanted to be independent. Because you didn't want to be a burden.

Penny nearly snorted in derision. How was that working out for her?

Somehow, she managed to push the door open and make the short walk to the workshop, but she was out of breath by the time she reached the door. Leaning against the wall, she bent over, resting her hands on her knees as a wave of dizziness rose up to overwhelm her. Somewhere in the distance, beyond the slightly ajar barn door, she could make out the faint strains of humming behind a steady whirring sound.

Matthew.

Penny gritted her teeth, fighting with all her might to stand upright again. Her present condition meant that she couldn't drag her feet, much as she might want to. She had to tell him now, or she might not get the chance. And she was *not* going to repeat the same mistake twice. No matter how badly it pained her now.

Willing her unsteady legs to move, she entered the shop, managing to make it to a rough-hewn wooden table before he caught sight of her.

"Penny?" The surprise that colored his gaze was swiftly replaced by concern. "What's wrong?"

Penny opened her mouth, but no words came. Instead, more tears. Instantly, he was at her side, enfolding her in his arms and murmuring reassuring words as he ran a comforting hand along her back. For a while, she clung to him, drawing from his strength and sobbing uncontrollably as the weight of the past few weeks overcame her.

Once she'd calmed down, Matthew drew back just enough so that he could look at her, then ran his thumb across her cheek, tenderly wiping away the last of her tears. "What happened, Penny? Is it about the contest?"

She swallowed hard and nodded, aware that she was still shaking and equally aware that there was absolutely nothing she could do about it. "Andrew," she choked out. "He b-basically fired me."

"What?" If she hadn't noticed the carefully restrained indignation hovering beneath his words, the way his arm tightened protectively around her would have told Penny exactly how he felt about the situation. "Why would he do that?"

She pressed her eyes shut, taking one last moment to prepare before telling him the truth. "I g-got a call… I have to leave."

He didn't say anything, but his entire body stilled. Heart heavy, she pressed on.

"It's not forever. B-but… I'll have to miss the contest."

"I don't understand," Matthew whispered. "Where are you going?"

She wanted to tell him, really she did. But it felt like a lead weight sat on her chest, stealing the air from her lungs and preventing her from speaking.

How could she tell him about her heart? After everything he had been through with Mac?

After everything she had been through with Nick?

A gentle finger under her chin brought her back to the present.

"Penny, look at me." He waited for her to oblige, then continued. "You can trust me. You know that, right?"

Still, she couldn't bring herself to speak. She wanted to believe him, but in the back of her mind, Nick's words rang like a tolling bell.

That's just not a risk I'm willing to take.

"When do you leave?" Matthew's subdued tone sliced through her heart like a dull knife. It was bad enough coming face-to-face with the hurt and disappointment in his eyes. It was downright torturous to know she'd put it there.

"Tonight."

He drew in a quick breath. "Wow."

Her thoughts exactly.

"But, you're coming back...?"

She met the hopeful glimmer in his eyes along with the question in his unfinished sentence. "I want to. Yes. But it might take some time."

He nodded, a tight gesture.

"I wanted you to know, this time," she whispered, her voice barely audible over the sound of her heart breaking. "Please don't be mad."

"Penny, I'm not mad at you." Those gentle words were like a salve for her weary soul. Relief coursed through her veins and weakened her already shaky knees. "Worried, yes, but never mad."

"I don't want you to worry about me."

One corner of his mouth hiked up into an adorable half smile. "Well, tough, because I do."

Penny chuckled in spite of herself. She hadn't realized she'd quoted herself from so many years ago. Only this time, Matthew couldn't step in and be her knight in shining armor.

"If only this was as easy as playing Lady Capulet," she sighed.

"I always thought you were more of a Juliet type."

Penny pulled a face.

"I never liked that story," she confessed.

"Me, neither." Matthew shrugged on a wink. "I was just trying to be romantic."

Penny laughed again, feeling her heavy heart lift when the sound coaxed his full smile out of hiding. "I think you do a good enough job of that all by yourself."

His expression changed, affection deepening into a knowing look that left her breathless. For several moments he held her gaze, the awareness between them stopping time.

"While we're sharing, there's something I want you to know, too."

Her heart throbbed in anticipation, its every beat feeling more and more laborious. Willing herself to focus on his words, she did her best to ignore it.

Just a little while longer.

"I don't know what's going on," he began, green eyes searching her face before returning to capture her gaze anew. "But I know that I don't want to lose you again. Of course, I want you to come back, but if you can't, I'll come to you. I'll find a way. We'll make it work."

Penny felt like she could barely breathe, much less think. Was this really happening?

"I care about you, Penny," Matthew declared. "As much more than just a friend. And I know you might not feel the same way, but—"

"No," she interrupted, not willing to let him believe that for even the briefest of moments. "I do care about you, Matthew. More than words can say."

Blinking fast against a fresh round of tears, she still couldn't clear her gaze enough to see him. Strong hands rising up to frame her face meant she didn't have to.

His lips touched hers, and she melted into his embrace. Safe and secure in the shelter of his arms, she lost herself in the moment.

Until...

Penny nearly cried out as a sharp flash of pain ripped through her chest. Pulling away, she drew in a ragged breath, pressing an unsteady hand over the place where her heart was straining to break free.

Not now...

"Penny? Are you okay?".

"M-my heart," she spluttered.

"Your heart?" Matthew asked, understandably confused. "It's safe with me, Penny, I promise. I meant every word I said."

"No, my *heart*," she whispered, eyes closing on a fresh wave of pain. "Like my mom's."

"I don't—" He froze, then terror struck as understanding dawned. "No. *No.*"

Oh, yes. And she was fading fast.

"Call...doctor..."

That was all she managed to say before everything turned to black.

"I can't believe it. I just can't believe it."

Andrew paced up and down the waiting room, his sentiment a carbon copy of the one reverberating through Matthew's head. Seated on an uncomfortable green vinyl chair, elbows resting on his knees with his hands clasped tight, he ran through the events of the morning.

How in the world had they ended up here? One minute Penny was in his arms, and the next, he was staring down at linoleum tile and breathing in the sharp smell of hospital antiseptic.

"This is all my fault," a nervous Andrew continued, hands now waving as he paced. "I fired my own sister. Who does that?"

"Someone who doesn't know the truth." The calm and soothing tone Morgan infused into her words perfectly juxtaposed Andrew's frantic energy. "Andy, relax. We're in a hospital. She's in good hands."

"How can you be so calm about this?" Andrew countered, turning on Morgan instead of heeding her words. "Why aren't you more shaken up?"

"Because she knew." The accusation flew out of Matthew's mouth before he could stop himself. But even without definitive proof, he knew that it was true. "Didn't you?"

A slight nod affirmed his suspicion.

"She told you and kept this from me?" Andrew blurted out. "Her own brother?"

"To be fair, Penny didn't initially want to tell me, either," Morgan explained. "And she didn't want to tell you because she knew that this would happen. She didn't want everyone freaking out and fussing over her. Or getting weirded out."

That last sentence was accompanied by a surreptitious glance in Matthew's direction. He took the less-than-subtle hint for what it was.

"She could have at least given us a chance," he said.

She could have given *him* a chance. On some level, he thought she had. But a secret like this…?

"It's too late for that now," Morgan somberly observed. "What's done is done. The only thing we can do now is pray."

Matthew agreed with that, at least. Now that he knew what was really going on, he wasn't going to leave her side. He'd stay here and pray tirelessly until they heard some good news, no matter how long that took.

"Aww, man." Refusing to be calmed by her suggestion, Andrew persisted in his one-man attempt to wear a hole through the floor. "All this over a stupid baking competition—that I forced her into. If I had known that she'd—"

Suddenly, he stopped, drew in a ragged breath, and raked his fingers through already messy hair as the truth of what he was saying finally sunk in. "What are we going to do if she..."

He didn't have to finish the question. The same one gnawed at Matthew with a horrifying intensity that threatened to throw him into an outright panic if he let himself think too hard about it.

Please, Lord, no. Not Penny, too.

"All right, that's enough out of you." Standing, Morgan grabbed hold of Andrew's shoulders. "Sit. Now."

She forced him down into a seat, but the now visibly drained Andrew didn't seem to need much convincing.

"Here's what we're going to do. First, we're going to stop thinking about the worst-case scenario and start thinking about what we'll do when Penny is out of surgery. And then you—" she threw a sharp finger point in Andrew's direction "—are going to go to your competition and win it for Penny."

"That's impossible," he protested. "How am I supposed to compete without a partner?"

"I can come with you," Matthew offered.

The lackluster expression on Andrew's face relayed his complete lack of confidence in the suggestion. "You?"

"Why not him?" Morgan queried. "Matthew's an expert on construction, and that's half the battle, isn't it?"

"I've been working behind the scenes with Penny for weeks

now," Matthew added on a noncommittal shrug. "I'm no expert, but I think I can handle it."

"But what about Penny?" Andrew's quiet question dampened their tenuous optimism. "We should be here, just in case…"

"Just in case what?" Morgan asked. "It's not like we can do anything for her here, other than wait and pray."

After a few moments of tense silence, Andrew finally spoke.

"If anything happens, you'd better call me right away."

"Of course."

"I mean it, Morgan," Andrew insisted. "I don't care if it's two minutes before the contest starts, if you get any news, you call me."

"I *will*," Morgan insisted with an eye roll that revealed their years' worth of friendship. "Now, get out of here. You've still got some time to prepare your new partner before you have to leave."

Andrew slanted his cool blue gaze at Matthew. "You ready for this?"

No, he thought, he wasn't ready. Not to face the possibility of life without Penny, and not to bake in her place, either. But what choice did he have but to keep going?

"As ready as I'll ever be."

The first thing Penny noticed was a rhythmic pulse, coming from somewhere far away.

Beep, beep, beep…

What was that? Her lids felt heavy as she struggled to open her eyes. Once she did, the harsh glare of fluorescent lights made her squint.

She tried to raise a hand to shield her face, but the movement stopped short on a wince when a new kind of pain radiated throughout her chest.

Forget the noise—what in the world was *that*?

"She's waking up!"

Was that Morgan? Where was she? The last Penny remembered, she had been with Matthew.

The collective gasp that followed her friend's announcement only confused Penny more.

"Hey, you." Morgan's voice was closer now, soft and soothing. "Try not to move too much just yet."

Finally, her eyes adjusted to the bright light, and Penny came face-to-face with a mixture of excited smiles and worried frowns.

"What…" She looked around, took in the sight of the bare hospital room, then tried to sit up. A stab of pain put an end to that.

"Careful, sweetheart." Nana slipped a small hand in hers and squeezed it tight, emotion thickening her usually lilting voice. "You need to rest."

"Why?" Her surroundings should have given away the answer, but Penny was still lost. "What happened?"

"You got rushed in for emergency surgery," Andrew explained, a sheepish look softening his angular features. "I'm so sorry, Penny. I had no idea. And what I said to you earlier…" Was that moisture she spied in his eyes? "It wasn't right. I was such a jerk. Can you ever forgive me?"

Now, she was the one tearing up. "Of course. But you're not the one who should be apologizing. I'm sorry, too. I never should have left you on your own after Mom died."

"No," Andrew protested. "I could have come, too, if I wanted." He hiked up a shoulder and paused. "I guess we both made a choice back then."

Penny nodded, a swell of relief, pride, and sisterly affection making her next words thick. "So we'll call it even, then?"

Andrew literally sidestepped the question by taking the

opportunity to move closer to Penny and hug her as much as he could manage with her in a hospital bed.

"Forget what I said," he murmured. "You're the best partner I could ever have. I love you, Penny."

"I love you too, Andy." She reached up as far as she could and returned his embrace. "And I'm so sorry about the contest."

When he pulled back, Penny was surprised to see him smiling at her. "Don't be. We won."

"What?" She gaped at him. "Wait, who's we?"

As if on cue, Matthew strode into the room, bearing a vase full to overflowing with colorful flowers. He stopped short when he saw her awake.

"This guy." Andrew jerked a thumb in Matthew's direction. "Completely saved the day. He managed to build an entire sleigh out of gingerbread, complete with decorative three-D cookie trim work!"

Penny arched an eyebrow. "Oh, really?"

"I may have picked up a thing or two by coaching you," Matthew responded humbly as he slipped past Andrew to place the flowers by her bed. "I thought you should have something beautiful to wake up to."

With that, Matthew leaned forward and dropped a tender kiss on her forehead.

"They're gorgeous." Penny smiled, basking in the warmth that radiated from his emerald gaze. "Thank you."

Matthew perched on the edge of the bed and draped an arm around her shoulder. Penny snuggled in close.

"I know we were joking about this before," he whispered. "But seriously, you can stop worrying me now. I think I've had enough excitement for a very long while."

Penny laughed, relief and contentment creating a heady mix of emotions. "I'll do my best."

"Your last-minute discovery was spot-on, by the way," Andrew continued, his excitement growing as he shared. "I don't think I've got the exact amount right just yet, but the judges loved the idea of including fresh ginger juice."

"I guess my secret's finally out," Nana sighed theatrically.

They chuckled, then Matthew nodded in Andrew's direction. "You haven't even told her the best part."

The best part? What could possibly top a first-place finish?

Andrew hesitated, an embarrassed smirk playing at the corners of his lips. "You remember that travel magazine I told you about? The one that was sponsoring the contest?"

"Yeah."

Penny's gaze flicked to Matthew, then Morgan, for clarification. Both were positively beaming.

"They offered me my own column."

"What? Are you serious?"

"I'm serious." Andrew's grin was broad now, a rare flush of color tinging his cheeks a pale pink. "They want me to share recipes and decorating tips in a monthly column. They credited my social-media feed for catching the editor's attention, so it's all thanks to you."

Penny's heart felt full to bursting. "Oh, Andy, I'm so happy for you! When do you start?"

"They're going to iron out the details and then send me a contract in the New Year," he said, his practiced nonchalance now returning after that brief reprieve. "Maybe you can help me brainstorm some ideas in the meantime."

"I'd love to."

"But not until after Christmas," Morgan chimed in. Then she addressed Penny. "We've got more news."

"More?" Penny marveled.

Morgan glanced at Nana, and immediately, Penny knew what she was about to say. "You sold the house."

"Yes," Nana replied. "I did."

Penny nodded slowly. She was surprised to find that she

didn't feel defeated. Or crushed. On the contrary, she felt a deeper peace beneath the surface, and with it, a conviction.

This is a good thing.

Penny was pleased to find that the smile she offered to her grandmother felt genuine. It was time to let go. Her mother's memories would live on in her heart, not a building. And surrounded by the love of her family and friends, Penny knew that it was these relationships, and not a house, that made her feel most at home.

"I'm happy for you, Nana. I really am."

"Thank you, dear," Nana replied. "But I think you'll be even happier when you find out who I sold it to."

Penny's lips twisted as she thought. Then her jaw went slack when Morgan, Andrew, and Matthew all pointed toward her.

"Me?"

"That's right." Morgan was practically glowing as she spoke.

"Matthew and I decided that we would use the prize money to buy Nana's house," Andrew explained. "It's our Christmas gift to you."

"But… That's too much," Penny protested. "I can't let you do that."

"We want to," Matthew insisted. "We know how much it means to you."

For several long moments, Penny couldn't speak. She could only smile, relieved tears welling in her eyes. She had always known her brother to be incredibly generous, but this took things to an entirely new level.

"I don't know what to say."

"I do," Andrew joked. "Say thank you."

Penny laughed, overwhelmed with gratitude. But something still didn't seem quite right to her.

"Okay," she finally said. "I'll accept your present. On one condition."

"What's that?" Andrew asked.

"That you allow me to regift it to Saving Grace."

Beside her brother, Morgan gasped. "You mean, the girls will have somewhere to go?"

"Sure," Penny replied. "They all need a fresh start, just like us. What better place to heal and start over again than Cedar Ridge?"

"Oh..." Morgan's eyes misted and her voice waned. She came closer and gave Penny a sideways hug. "This is just incredible. Thank you, Penny. I can't wait to call Anne."

A peace she'd never known before settled over Penny's heart. "It looks like you were right, Morgan," she said. "God did provide. Things always work out when you put your trust in Him."

"Amen to that," her friend concurred.

A couple of quick knocks on the door caught their attention. "Sorry to interrupt."

A young man stood in the doorway, a blue file folder in hand. He didn't seem to be much older than herself, but there was no mistaking the white lab coat and stethoscope hanging around his neck.

"I'm Dr. Calloway," the man introduced himself, all business as he strode up to the bed. "If it's all right with you, I'd like to discuss the results of your operation."

He slid his gaze around the room, silently asking for Penny's permission to continue.

"We can leave if you want," Morgan offered.

Penny shook her head. "No, please stay. I'm done with keeping secrets."

"That's good," Andrew retorted. "Because I wasn't planning on going anywhere."

A quick squeeze of her shoulder confirmed Matthew's agreement. "Neither was I."

"We're all in this together, sweetheart," Nana chimed in. "And we'll help in whatever way we can."

Penny scanned the room, silently thanking God for the wonderful people He placed in her life. Whatever the outcome, with her friends and family by her side, Penny felt ready to face anything.

"Okay." She addressed Dr. Calloway with a quick nod. "I'm ready."

"All right," he began as he opened the file folder and began to peruse its contents. "So according to your records, you were diagnosed with hypertrophic cardiomyopathy several weeks ago, correct?"

"Yes." Penny swallowed past the lump that had risen in her throat. Whatever Dr. Calloway was about to say, she resolved to accept as being God's will. But she still hoped for good news.

"Well, Ms. Shay," the doctor continued, redirecting his dark-eyed gaze to hers. "It appears as if you were misdiagnosed."

Penny froze, wondering if she had heard Dr. Calloway correctly. Beside her, she heard Matthew suck in a quick breath.

"I'm sorry?" she asked.

"You don't simply have hypertrophic cardiomyopathy," Dr. Calloway explained, closing the folder with a quick snap. "You have *obstructive* hypertrophic cardiomyopathy."

Casting a glance around the room, Penny was met with worried expressions and deep frowns. Clearly, everyone was thinking the same thing she was: That didn't sound a whole lot better.

"Simply put," Dr. Calloway continued, "your heart muscles *are* thickened. But not enough to cause serious impairment."

"So…" Penny began, thoroughly confused. "What's been causing all these problems?"

"One section of heart tissue is thicker than the rest," Dr. Calloway went on. "Over time, it began to push itself into one of your heart's chambers. The occasional blockage was preventing the blood from flowing, and that was the cause of your symptoms. But they shouldn't be bothering you anymore, now that we've removed it."

Penny closed her eyes, hoping against hope with every fiber of her being. "So, if you removed the blockage...does this mean I'm cured?"

"Well, I wouldn't necessarily say that," the doctor hedged. "The muscles of your heart *are* thicker than most, and at some point, they could pose a serious risk to your health, so we'll have to stay vigilant and monitor it."

"But I'm going to be fine?" Penny persisted.

Tiny lines appeared around Dr. Calloway's eyes as he finally allowed himself to smile at Penny.

"Yes, Ms. Shay, you're going to be just fine."

Chapter Eleven

Between preparing for the grand opening and getting Nana's house ready for the Saving Grace ladies' arrival, the next week passed in a flurry of activity. Penny, of course, was relegated to the sidelines by her well-meaning yet overprotective clan, but despite the occasional protest, she was happy to be cared for by the people she loved.

By the time the six women and their darling children arrived, just two days before Christmas, the large Colonial had been filled with every kind of festive holiday knickknack and decoration known to man. Gifts had been wrapped, stockings hung, and a delicious feast planned for the occasion. Weary from the journey, the sight was a welcome reprieve for the new residents, who had yet to stop thanking them for their generosity.

Seated at the long table where so many family celebrations had been centered in the past, Penny couldn't remember a more joy-filled Christmas. Contented smiles brightened the room as the carefree laughter of children delighting in their Christmas treasures rang in the background.

Could this get any better?

No, Penny imagined that she couldn't possibly feel more blessed than she did right now.

Close on the heels of that thought came a profound awareness of God's immense goodness. Transforming her childhood home into a haven for these women and children was so much greater than anything she could have imagined when Penny first resolved to purchase the home herself.

Lord, You are so good to us.

"Are you ready?" Matthew asked her. "I can't wait any longer to give you your present."

"Of course." Penny greeted him with her warmest smile, her voice as soft as the kiss she pressed to his cheek. "But you do know that you're the only Christmas present I need, right?"

A mysterious little glint danced in his emerald gaze. "Why don't you wait until you find out what it is first?"

Penny drew a finger along the strong line of his jaw, wondering at his cryptic comment. "Trying to pique my curiosity, Mr. Banks?"

"Only if it's working, Miss Shay."

Taking her hand, he led her to the front room by the Christmas tree, now bereft of the multitude of colorfully wrapped boxes that had surrounded it that morning.

"Do you need to sit down?"

Penny couldn't contain an amused smile as Matthew's eyes darted between the couch and the bay window, searching for the perfect seat. "Matthew, I'm fine. Between you, Andrew, and Nana, I feel like all I've done is sit for the last two weeks."

An apologetic laugh escaped him. "I guess we have gone a little overboard."

She tipped her head to the side in jest. "You think?"

Another laugh made her stomach flip-flop. "Well, hopefully this will make it up to you."

He stepped around the Christmas tree, disappearing momentarily to retrieve a small box. Penny took the opportunity to draw in a slow and steady breath, her every nerve humming with anticipation.

"I've been thinking lately that there's something missing from this tree," he began.

"Oh?" That was the last thing she had expected to hear.

"Yeah, but I found the perfect ornament to make up for it." Handing her the box, he asked, "Would you do the honors?"

Penny accepted the offering and turned toward the tree. It was already jammed full of Christmas decorations. She couldn't imagine what Matthew might have found to add to the mix. Absentmindedly lifting the lid off the box, she scanned the loaded branches, searching for an opening. But once she pulled out the ornament, Penny stopped short on a gasp.

The wooden ornament was simple, but its shape was unmistakable.

An engagement ring?

When she turned around for an explanation, Penny found Matthew kneeling down to offer her the real thing.

Was this really happening?

"Penelope Shay," Matthew began, his hopeful smile a perfect complement to the reverent adoration shining in his gaze. "I love you. In fact, I think I've always loved you. Must have been that elf costume."

An unexpected gurgle of laughter caught her off guard. "You're terrible," she chided, swiping at the tears that threatened to obscure her vision with trembling hands. "But I love you, too, Matthew. So much."

"These last few weeks have been the happiest of my life," he continued. "And that's all because of you. Now that you're home, now that we're together, I don't ever want to lose you again."

Penny shook her head. "You won't." And she meant it. Penny never intended to leave again. She belonged here, in Cedar Ridge. With him.

"Penny, will you marry me?"

Matthew got blurry as a fresh round of tears welled in her eyes. "Yes."

In an instant, strong arms wrapped themselves around her,

lifting Penny off the ground and twirling her around in a celebratory spin. When he set her down, Matthew kissed her, a kiss that held the promise of forever.

"I don't know how I'm supposed to follow that up," Penny joked once he pulled away.

Matthew's brow furrowed in the most adorable way. "What do you mean?"

"I have something for you, too," Penny smiled.

"You didn't need to get me anything." He pressed a kiss to her forehead, then another on her nose. "Your *yes* is the only present I need."

Penny beamed under his affection. "Well, consider this a bonus, then."

Mathew chuckled. "Okay."

"Do you remember when I told you about my museum-hopping days?" she asked.

"Yes." Matthew grinned. "I'll be keeping an eye out for it during the next Olympics."

"Well, I got to know some of the curators in my time away," Penny continued, too excited to share her news to acknowledge his teasing. "Once I finished your website, I sent it to some friends in Manhattan. One of them sent back inquiring about setting up an exhibit at The Miller Art Gallery."

Matthew froze. "You mean..."

Penny nodded. "If you agree to the terms, Mac's artwork will be on display this May."

"You're kidding!"

"Nope."

"Penny, this is incredible! Thank you!"

His arms tightened to draw her close once again, and Penny reveled in the feeling.

"So what do you think?" Matthew asked overhead. "Should we go to New York for our honeymoon?"

Penny leaned back to meet his gaze. "You really think we can plan a wedding in a matter of months?"

"Why not?" Matthew shrugged. "This Christmas has taught me that anything is possible."

She couldn't agree more. Penny never could have imagined how much her life would change in a few short weeks. And she was beyond grateful that it did.

"Okay," she agreed. "A May wedding, then."

A teasing smile edged up his lips. "Do we have a deal?"

"We do."

And they sealed it with a kiss.

* * * * *

Dear Reader,

The Christmas season offers us many beautiful truths to contemplate. For me, the most awe-inspiring has always been that the God who holds the world in his hands would choose to enter into that same world, not as a powerful ruler, but as a helpless, dependent child. What a beautiful example of trust and dependence!

Penny and Matthew also had to learn to trust. Firstly, that God was not only in control of their lives, but that He loves them and doesn't hold their past mistakes against them. Then came the hard task of trusting each other, of choosing to hope for and pursue their second chance. Trust can be scary, but love is always worth the risk!

Thank you for choosing to pick up *Her Second Chance Christmas!*

Wishing you and your families a blessed and joyful Christmas season,

Isabella Bruno

Get up to 4 Free Books!

We'll send you 2 free books from each series you try PLUS a free Mystery Gift.

FREE Value Over $25

Both the **Love Inspired®** and **Love Inspired® Suspense** series feature compelling novels filled with inspirational romance, faith, forgiveness and hope.

YES! Please send me 2 FREE novels from the Love Inspired or Love Inspired Suspense series and my FREE gift (gift is worth about $10 retail). After receiving them, if I don't wish to receive any more books, I can return the shipping statement marked "cancel." If I don't cancel, I will receive 6 brand-new Love Inspired Larger-Print books or Love Inspired Suspense Larger-Print books every month and be billed just $7.19 each in the U.S. or $7.99 each in Canada. That is a savings of 20% off the cover price. It's quite a bargain! Shipping and handling is just 50¢ per book in the U.S. and $1.25 per book in Canada.* I understand that accepting the 2 free books and gift places me under no obligation to buy anything. I can always return a shipment and cancel at any time by calling the number below. The free books and gift are mine to keep no matter what I decide.

Choose one:
- ☐ **Love Inspired Larger-Print** (122/322 BPA G36Y)
- ☐ **Love Inspired Suspense Larger-Print** (107/307 BPA G36Y)
- ☐ **Or Try Both!** (122/322 & 107/307 BPA G36Z)

Name (please print)

Address   Apt. #

City   State/Province   Zip/Postal Code

Email: Please check this box ☐ if you would like to receive newsletters and promotional emails from Harlequin Enterprises ULC and its affiliates. You can unsubscribe anytime.

Mail to the Harlequin Reader Service:
IN U.S.A.: P.O. Box 1341, Buffalo, NY 14240-8531
IN CANADA: P.O. Box 603, Fort Erie, Ontario L2A 5X3

Want to explore our other series or interested in ebooks? Visit www.ReaderService.com or call 1-800-873-8635.

---

*Terms and prices subject to change without notice. Prices do not include sales taxes, which will be charged (if applicable) based on your state or country of residence. Canadian residents will be charged applicable taxes. Offer not valid in Quebec. This offer is limited to one order per household. Books received may not be as shown. Not valid for current subscribers to the Love Inspired or Love Inspired Suspense series. All orders subject to approval. Credit or debit balances in a customer's account(s) may be offset by any other outstanding balance owed by or to the customer. Please allow 4 to 6 weeks for delivery. Offer available while quantities last.

Your Privacy—Your information is being collected by Harlequin Enterprises ULC, operating as Harlequin Reader Service. For a complete summary of the information we collect, how we use this information and to whom it is disclosed, please visit our privacy notice located at https://corporate.harlequin.com/privacy-notice. Notice to California Residents – Under California law, you have specific rights to control and access your data. For more information on these rights and how to exercise them, visit https://corporate.harlequin.com/california-privacy. For additional information for residents of other U.S. states that provide their residents with certain rights with respect to personal data, visit https://corporate.harlequin.com/other-state-residents-privacy-rights/.

LIRLIS25